EX LIBRIS

VINTAGE CLASSICS

COPI

Born in Buenos Aires in 1939, Raúl Damonte Botana derived his sobriquet Copi from a nickname his grandmother gave him, 'copito de nieve', or 'little snowflake'. At six, he went into exile with his family in Uruguay and eventually settled in Paris, where he was a cartoonist, performer, playwright and novelist until his death from an AIDS-related illness in 1987.

KIT SCHLUTER

Kit Schluter is the author of *Cartoons* and has recently translated books from the French and Spanish by bruno darío, Rafael Bernal, Mario Levrero, Marcel Schwob, Olivia Tapiero and Enrique Vila-Matas. He lives in Mexico City.

ALSO BY COPI

The Queen's Ball

COPI
CITY OF RATS

TRANSLATED FROM THE FRENCH BY
Kit Schluter

WITH AN INTRODUCTION BY
César Aira

VINTAGE CLASSICS

1 3 5 7 9 10 8 6 4 2

Vintage Classics is part of the Penguin Random House group of companies

Vintage, Penguin Random House UK, One Embassy Gardens,
8 Viaduct Gardens, London SW11 7BW

penguin.co.uk/vintage-classics
global.penguinrandomhouse.com

This edition published in Vintage Classics in 2026
This edition first published in the United States of America by New Directions in 2026

Copyright © 1979 by the Literary Estate of Copi
Translation copyright © 2026 by Kit Schluter
Introduction copyright © César Aira 1988

The moral right of the author has been asserted

Penguin Random House values and supports copyright. Copyright
fuels creativity, encourages diverse voices, promotes freedom of expression
and supports a vibrant culture. Thank you for purchasing an authorised edition
of this book and for respecting intellectual property laws by not reproducing,
scanning or distributing any part of it by any means without permission. You are
supporting authors and enabling Penguin Random House to continue to publish
books for everyone. No part of this book may be used or reproduced in any
manner for the purpose of training artificial intelligence technologies or systems.
In accordance with Article 4(3) of the DSM Directive 2019/790, Penguin Random
House expressly reserves this work from the text and data mining exception.

Printed and bound in Great Britain by Clays Ltd, Elcograf S.p.A.

The authorised representative in the EEA is Penguin Random House Ireland,
Morrison Chambers, 32 Nassau Street, Dublin D02 YH68

A CIP catalogue record for this book is available from the British Library

ISBN 9781529951523

Penguin Random House is committed to a sustainable future
for our business, our readers and our planet. This book is made
from Forest Stewardship Council® certified paper.

Contents

Introduction by César Aira   ix

Notice   3
Translator's preface   5
The Young Rat   7
The Surprise Party   12
The Queen of Rats   18
The Human Child   27
The Periscope   30
The Bat, the Fox Terrier, and the Bees   35
Vidvn   41
Mimile   45
The Capture   51
The Snake   55
The Pieces of Evidence   59
The Ecological God   64
The Rat Devil   69
The Emir of Parrots   74
The Rat Orator   80
The Atheist Rat   89
Disneyland   95
The Magic Mushrooms   103
The City of Rats   108
The Return to Land   115
Translator's afterword   121

Introduction

COPI, WHOSE GIVEN NAME WAS RAÚL DAMONTE (BUENOS Aires, 1940–Paris, 1987), was a cartoonist, novelist, playwright and actor. He was Argentine, Uruguayan, French, and Italian. He was a great artist (a great among the greatest) but he used his genius to carve out a marginal place for himself, where he could be mistaken for a nonartist, a dilettante. He was highly undefined, which is why he could do everything. He didn't know how to do anything, which is why he could be anything he wanted. But he didn't desire anything, which is why he could pierce through all the membranes of reality and fiction, of life and death. He was not a Frenchman born in Argentina, nor an Argentine exiled in France, nor a Franco-Argentine acting in Italian, nor an Italian in Uruguay.

He was, at the outset, an illustrator who did not know how to draw, and who drew wonderfully. "It took me my whole life to learn to draw like a child," Picasso once said. He was referring to a discontinuity between art and art, which makes it impossible for ordinary people. It is miraculous when a human being makes the leap and becomes an artist. That leap, that miracle, was the life of Copi, who didn't know how to write, neither in French nor in Spanish, of course, and yet he wrote some of the most beautiful books in either language: *L'Uruguayen* (The Uruguayan), *Le bal des folles* (*The Queens' Ball*), *La cité des rats* (*City of Rats*), *La vida es un tango* (Life is a tango). His entire body of work is marked by a lack of memory. He is like Isak Dinesen, who once, when dictating a novel, made a character appear who had died chapters before. When her secretary pointed this out to her, the baroness replied: "My dear, that is of no importance whatsoever." In Copi, each page is forgotten with the arrival of the next. Here's the thing: Copi himself forgot that he couldn't write or draw. After all, what is there between a thing and its memory if not time? And *that* can never appear in a drawing. (Time is the archaeological remnant of an old sentimental literature that no longer moves us.)

With theater, the story was a bit different. Because the world is a theater, at least for a Baroque man, and Copi was a Baroque man—a Shakespeare, a Calderón, magically reincarnated in gay Paris. That the theater contained the world, and vice versa, was a natural necessity of the same system of transformations that made him child and adult, artist and nonartist, man and woman. And also alive and dead, because he knew how to make death itself participate in his method of transformations and reversibilities. In one of his best plays, *Les quatres jumelles* (*The Four Twins*), the characters die and are reborn about twenty times each, and it's perfectly plausible.

Because Copi was not a surrealist, or an absurdist, or a magician. He was a realist, except that he worked with drawings, and he didn't know how to draw. Children don't know *how* to draw; they know what they *want* to draw. They want to draw, for example, a spaceship with the computer out of sync because of the laser beam shot at it by a magnetic King Kong aboard a pirate galleon that has been attacked by a panda shark with two nephews, one good and one bad. They are able to draw because they don't know how. Children, like accomplished artists, are possessed of a positive and free will. It's not omnipotence, it is reality, plain and simple, life accepted as a process of becoming. The great Yes of a new style of Renaissance man. Becoming has desubstantialized the world, has stripped it of all its significations, has transformed it into a life—into Copi's exemplary lives.

If we do not recognize at first glance the world-life that is art, it is because its dimensions are different. Space-time is a maquette. Copi is the greatest miniaturist of our time; everything happens on a small canvas the size of the eye, and very quickly. In general, critics agree that reading Copi draws us in, engulfs us, but not all of them point out that, before this irresistible impulse, there is a transposition to the microscopic, or rather subatomic, level. There we find once more the vicissitudes of our existence, but organized in a new way. Heisenberg's principle provides an explanation: there is a state so small that qualities cease to apply to things, and it all begins to float freely, qualities and things, as well as time, place, relationships, perception, as in a democratic family reunion. That is called the "uncertainty principle," but only because the observer continues to believe he is Gulliver in Lilliput. Copi generalizes, and so do we, when we become Copi (and we have no choice but to do so); we float on the same level as everything else, and our dreams, fingers, desires, hair, ideas, clothes, memories, certainties and uncertainties, near or far, do too.

CÉSAR AIRA

City Of Rats

Notice

THE AUTHOR AND EDITOR REFER ALL GRAMMAR AND syntax maniacs, readers drunk on tense agreement, imperfect subjunctive addicts, fabricators of internal-use-only neologisms, semicolon nitpickers, and other such fanatics of Littré, Robert, or Grévisse back to their preferred reading materials.

Translator's preface

I BECAME ACQUAINTED WITH THE LETTERS THAT MAKE up this account two years after the final one had been signed. They had traveled a long way from one post office to the other: our dear rat had written "Icubedeur 61" on the envelope, my address being 19 Rue de Buci, because rats see things inverted in comparison to humans, and when they learn to transform their thoughts into literature (it's more common than you'd think) they flip the whole phrase, and its decryption is not always a simple matter, although I think I've managed to the best of my ability here, even if certain passages penned in the rats' language (two or three entire paragraphs of nothing but the letter *i*, for example) fell away under my ruthless scissors. As for the title, if the author had suspected that his letters would ever be published, he'd have decided on one himself. *Letters from a Rat* struck me as distasteful to utter and *The Wonderful World of Rats* smacked of ecoprotest, so I decided on *City of Rats*, perhaps because I detect in Gouri's writings hints of an influence from a book I read aloud to him back in his youth: Dickens's *A Tale of Two Cities*. I hope you take as much pleasure in reading these letters as I took in their decryption. And with that, dear readers: all my best, as they say,

Copi

The Young Rat

DEAR MASTER: I GOT WORD THAT YOU BROKE THREE ribs, which must be why I haven't seen you wheeling your little shopping bag around the Carrefour de Buci lately. It must not be much fun up there on the fifth floor without an elevator, though thankfully you have a TV and that Portuguese woman who shops and cleans for you every Sunday morning. I can't come up to visit you anymore because the concierge spotted me. I've found lodgings more suitable than my previous trash can, at the florist's (the blonde woman with the husky voice) on the corner of Rue Grégoire-de-Tours, right next to the bar-tabac with the yellow painted mailbox. My lodgings are, admittedly, modest. I dug a tunnel down into the root system of a succulent and piled up some thistles for a cot. To go out, I camouflage myself in a not-too-wet bouquet of tulips and wander the shelves, nibbling on whatever strikes my fancy (she has some sublime white chrysanthemums), and as soon as my belly's full, vroom! back to my hole for a nap. So don't worry about me. I've got bed and board. As for the rest . . . I'm making the best of it. I may have felt safer tucked up in your slippers, but I've tried sneaking up to your apartment twice recently: the first time, the concierge threw a bucket of paint at me, which I narrowly avoided as it splashed all over the landing, sending her into a rage; the second, a jar of mustard gave me the scar I still wear between my two ears. I insisted no more, all the while lamenting those times when, to get me up to your two-room flat, you would hide me in your wheeled shopping bag and she was none the wiser. Later on, I did try to sneak in a third time, in the small hours when I heard her snoring, but a cat leapt treacherously upon me (in the meantime, that viper had procured herself a Persian Longhair); I bit her ear, which drove her back, but I scurried off posthaste because she's young and swift of paw. Since then, I haven't dared tempt fate. Here at the florist's the scene is certainly colorful, but how I miss those days when I slept all cozy and warm on the corner of your pillow while you read me comic books, dear Master! I'm dropping this letter into the yellow box, with a green stamp I stole from the bar-tabac while the lady was distracted; I hope you won't be upset by its brevity. From now on, I'll write you longer letters, I promise. Take good care of your broken ribs. Your dear rat.

Postscriptum. I'm reopening the letter to add some recent news: my situation has markedly improved now that I've joined forces with one of my fellow rats named Rakä who, though young, has already traveled the whole world round in the hull of a Venezuelan cargo ship. He's a stocky little one-and-a-half-year-old from Madeira, the son of a guinea pig and a white mouselet; he blends his father's imposing physique with the red eyes and finesse of his mother, whose ancestors were sacred animals in Madeira before the arrival of striped tomcats, which the Portuguese sailors introduced along with fleas. Rakä may not be as book smart as you, but he's better acquainted with the world and its ways. He lives four stories under La Vieille France, that little patisserie right beside your building, where he has squatted a splendid catacomb-era duplex, decorating its skulls with souvenirs from his travels: a Zulu coin, an Aztec scarf, and a gramophone needle he picked up on the Isle of Manhattan, which all goes to show the extent of his travels. He turned me on to opium, and has a great ball of the stuff which he brought back from Amsterdam. When night falls, we lounge on two skulls and, between puffs, he describes to me in detail the Iguazu Falls, the Strait of Magellan, and the Amazon Delta, which, as everyone knows, are the three natural wonders of this world. What grandiose reveries for me, I who have known but slums and have ventured just once along the gutter of Rue de Seine, only to see the oily banks of the river of the same name! Often, I spend the night at Rakä's in his spare bed: a clear plastic bag of multicolor cotton balls. But don't go thinking that we spend our days lost in daydreams; we spend most of our time on our already thriving business venture: We catch earthworms at the florist's on the corner of Rue Grégoire-de-Tours and bread them in the sacks of flour they leave lying around La Vieille France. Once the worms suffocate to death, we offer them up to the pigeons that are always pecking around on the corner of Rue de Seine where we have a stand on a blue three-egg polystyrene carton, right at the mouth of the sewer that's in front of the greengrocer at the crossing of Rue de Buci. We don't make much—the pigeons have nothing more to spend than the five centime coins they find lying on the ground (they're always confusing them with cuff links or even gold cigarette filters)—but it's enough to lead a sweet life free of need, and, besides, it's a pleasure to work with Rakä, who always has some witticism on his lips and knows how to keep a conversation going with the pigeons, chatting them up about the weather as I ring open the cash register we contrived in an earring we nicked from the supermarket. Today, a human died in your building; I hope it wasn't you. In any event, I'll post this letter off tonight, in the hope that you didn't die of worry after not hearing from me for so long. Sincerely yours, your dear rat who thinks the world of you.

Dear master: Fortunately, it wasn't you who died; your initials weren't the ones on the bouquet of orchids the corner florist prepared while crying her eyes out, the slain was her mother, who lived, it would seem, in the chambre de bonne above your apartment. I wanted to take advantage of the pandemonium on Rue de Buci (every shopkeeper in the neighborhood came by to buy at least one bouquet of white roses from the florist for her mother) to sneak into your apartment, but the concierge's cat is still posted up at the landing, flashing her claws. From your sickbed, you must have heard the mother's coffin making a racket as it banged against the stairway walls (it took them an hour to get it all the way down); and here's what happened next: Just when they got the coffin out to the courtyard, the daughter (the blonde florist with the hoarse voice) exploded at the undertakers, accusing them of damaging a handle, the concierge accuses them of having scratched the banister; the undertakers, who were expecting their tip, storm off and leave the coffin in the middle of the courtyard. It's almost four p.m. already, everyone who had been invited to the funeral goes back to open up their shops, the coffin is inserted vertically into a dumpster and leaned against a wall where it will await the black garbagemen who will come take it away at sunrise, even if only to steal its handles, tossing the corpse into a dumpster along with the orchids and the trash. Then an argument broke out between the concierge and the florist (whose dearly departed mother owed her a holiday bonus). I'll never know who had the last word because the Persian Longhair leapt treacherously upon me and bit my tail while I was distracted by the scene. I was able to break free from her claws and I returned to the sewer in the blink of an eye, where I wrapped my tail with a Band-Aid I found lying around. At your feet, Master. Your DEAR RAT. (Translated by Copi.)

The Surprise Party

DEAR MASTER: I HOPE YOU'VE RECEIVED MY PREVIOUS missives, though I'm beginning to lose hope that I'll ever see you ambling around the Carrefour de Buci again. It's been nearly three months since you broke three ribs wheeling your shopping bag down the stairs.

Spring has sprung. Rakä and I sunbathe on the Tuileries' first primroses; Paris is beautiful this time of year. We crafted two bathing suits out of some blue jeans we snipped with our teeth at the dry cleaner's and, every Sunday morning, instead of opening "The Olde Wormery" (that's the name we gave to our breaded worm stand), we stroll Rue Dauphine and go for a picnic on the Square du Vert-Galant with a host of our fellow rats who also managed to elude the icy fangs of winter. We paddle around for a while in the Seine's warm water, taking care not to get nipped by the monkfish, then lie ourselves down on a washcloth laid out on a cobblestone, and we take our sunbath — so precious to a rat's health. The fur we lost on our backs and tails from a bout with mange starts to grow back, silky and gray, and our whiskers, limp from the frosty winter gutters, stand erect again, reddish and haughty, on either side of our muzzles. We bring our lunch: chipboard canapés sprinkled with pumpkin seeds, which we wash down with a cocktail whose recipe Rakä brought back from the Hawaiian islands: one drop of vinegar, one of motor oil, and avocado pit zest; it's scrumptious, even if it goes straight to the head, especially this spring, which has been exceptionally sunny for Paris according to the older rats among us. We made the acquaintance of two young females, Iris and Carina, daughters from the same litter, whose father, once a successful frozen carrot peel merchant in Rungis, where he recently died, crushed by a butcher's truck, left them a splendid property you're sure to have noticed on your strolls over the Pont des Arts: the willow tree on the western tip of the Île de la Cité. We met them swimming; Iris (who's small and pink, practically hairless) had slipped and didn't know how to swim, so Rakä dove bravely in to her rescue and carried her back to the riverbank by the scruff of her neck while I tried to resuscitate Carina, who had fainted beside me as soon as she saw her sister in danger. To make matters worse, Iris's cries caught the attention of a human policeman with a brutish face who charged us, holding up his billy club, but the four of us darted into the willow roots, leaving the cop outside, kicking at the tree. We're well aware that swimming in the Seine is forbidden to humans, but there's no signage forbidding it to rats, and Carina wasted no time in writing a spirited complaint to the chief of police, however well we know from past experience that nothing ever comes of such procedures.

Soon they sent us away, claiming to be seriously behind on their correspondence, but inviting us for dinner at the next sunrise, as is customary among Parisians of good taste. We were made to understand that formal attire was required for the occasion. So we bolted over to the toy store on Rue Guénégaud and climbed into the outfits of the two Mickeys in the window: a green jacket, tartan trousers, a little white silk scarf, and a cap for Rakä; a purple velvet suit, a mustard yellow ruffled silk shirt, and an opera hat for me. We arrived at the Square du Vert-Galant around five a.m., both of us wheezing from dragging two bouquets of violets the length of the Rue Dauphine gutter. Iris and Carina were awaiting us, seated on the willow roots in the early morning light, wrapped in tunics; Iris, with her yellow eyes, black whiskers, and thick tuft of red hair on her right ear, wore one of pale yellow toilet paper, and Carina, who is burgundy from head to toe except for her albino snout and tail, wore a pleated pink Kleenex. Their valet, a hamster decked out in a French Tickler around his neck and Coca-Cola cap atop his head, served us thimbles of consommé in the willow's canopy, up on the balcony, which had a magnificent view of the barges that glide over the Seine, parting the bunches of drifting orange peels. The human river firefighters performed an aquatic parade under the Pont des Arts, which we found truly delightful and applauded wildly. Iris, a bit tipsy, lifted the toilet paper, revealing her hind legs, and danced a few steps on the willow branches to the rhythm her sister Carina rapped out clumsily with her claws upon an oyster fork. To tell you the truth, dear Master, the fact is that I find Iris more enticing than Carina, even if Carina has made her intentions clear to me by licking her whiskers every time her albino eyes alight upon my fly. Suddenly, a serpentine wind shook the willow's branches and we tumbled to the ground; we made the most of it and went down into the salon under the roots, where a fine blueberry casserole awaited us, served by the same hamster as before, though now he was wearing a chef's toque carved out of a radish. Carina settled down to my left, Rakä across from me, and Iris in fourth place at a table made of a cheese board over which four egg cups towered like thrones and in which we sat most elegantly, wrapping our tails around them. It was Carina who served the delectable pot of blueberries while regaling us with the recipe: dip a snail in a cup of coarse salt until it's nice and dry, slice the snail into very thin slivers and sauté them, tossing in some of the coarse salt, let it all burn, and stuff the snail's charred remains into a head of garlic which, in the end, only serves to add flavor to a plastic cup of blueberry yogurt, which we pour out over the cheese board: it's exquisite, everyone dives right in in search of the garlic. Our brand-new clothes are quickly drenched in yogurt, and that's when the two sisters take the opportunity to get us erect, brushing our whiskers with their tails, and Iris, like it was nothing, starts coupling with Rakä, choking him to make him ejaculate, while Carina does the same to me, inserting a claw into my anus. This scene lasted but a few seconds, after which we discretely resumed our places at the table, dabbing at the yogurt with our napkins. Just then, we heard the footsteps of the hamster who, this time, was bringing us a candied beetle served upon his very own toque. He flambéed it with a match before our eyes and backed away into a tunnel, bowing to us on his way out.

Rakä and I were getting ready to dig into the beetle when Iris complained of a stomach ache, crying pregnancy, and Carina soon followed her sister's example. Rakä and I tried to assure them of our good intention to marry, but they insulted us, calling us commoners and rakes. They cried out for the hamster and ordered him to go wake their mother to inform her of the rape they had just suffered in their own villa at the hands of these two young bathers from the public beach. The hamster screeched with fright and leapt through a trapdoor; Rakä and I exchanged a knowing wink and made a break for the main exit, toppling the furniture behind us. That's when a horde of hamsters armed with toothpicks and mustard-pot-lid shields burst out of every tunnel, blocking our path while the wail of a siren exploded into the chamber as a red fire truck hurtled at full speed down a ramp and crashed into the cheese plate, scattering the leftovers of our feast, its four wheels coming to a complete stop after a slow agony in the air. This accident caused a stir among the hamsters, who began talking very quickly in their language amongst themselves. Suddenly, someone appeared: a great female rat dressed in authentic human skin, stretched extremely tight all over, with a safety pin stuck through her snout and her hind legs stuffed into shrimp shells, dropped down heavily from a hole in the ceiling onto the fire truck, seriously denting the hood, before she squealed: "Whose red vehicle is this?" A deathly silence fell over her audience, which was soon cut short by the sobs of the two girls, Iris and Carina. "Shut your mouths, you little bastards," shrieked the enormous female, and they fell silent. This peremptory tone assured us that this was their mother, the frozen carrot peel merchant's widow. "I've said it before and I'll say it again: I don't take kindly to unseemly objects in my salon! Get it out of my sight at once," she commanded the hamster army, kicking her shrimp shell against one of the truck's wheels, which began to spin as if of its own volition. The hamsters conferred privately before one of them answered curtly: "We want a raise, Madame," then he coughed. "I've already granted you usufruct of the dead mackerels floating on the Seine!" "But so many of us drown while fishing for them," offered an energetic voice from deep in a tunnel, "you should be buying us cork floaters and yards of sewing thread to tie to the willow branches so those waves from the barges don't sweep us away!" "A good lot of us crack our skulls on the piling of the Pont des Arts," said a nasally voice. "That's how I lost my neighbor here in the burrow," a voice added. "This is mutiny!" the enormous female wailed. And speaking for the first time to Rakä and me: "With you, sirs, as my witnesses!" "But they're our prisoners!" protested the hamster we recognized as the army's leader because he wore a golden cider cap on his head while the others had only clear white plastic wine caps. "Never mind, they'll be prisoners and witnesses at the same time," said the enormous female, as she came trotting toward us.

The Queen of Rats

"ALLOW ME TO INTRODUCE MYSELF," SHE SAID, COQUETT-ishly wagging her lipstick-smeared mustache, "I'm the Queen of Darkness, but you can call me Bijou. Bow wow!" she wailed, barking like a dog and nudging us with her elbow. "So, you're the ones who raped my daughters, are you?" she asked. "You must have strong stomachs." And she roared with laughter, a laughter that infected the entire army. Carina and Iris, humiliated by their mother, shook with anger and stared at us with bloodshot eyes, not daring to take a step toward us. With this little quip, the Queen had won back her troops. "Tonight, you'll be getting *two* peanuts for your hors-d'oeuvres!" she cried out to the hamsters. Some applause and whistling echoed around the enclosure. Taking Rakä and me each by an arm, she said, "Let's go out for some fresh air on the aircraft carrier, and let this little crew plan its mutiny!" A number of hamsters blocked our passage, calling us sellouts, but we reached the roots' opening untouched.

Over the Square du Vert-Galant shined the May sun, the kind that makes you squint with pleasure when you see it reflecting off the surface of waters over which skate butterflies of myriad colors. The aircraft carrier consisted of a vegetable crate bobbing near the bank, lashed to the root of the willow tree with a rope that doubled as the gangway; atop the crate, a mast pilfered from the Samaritaine's toy department stood between two boards. Hanging upside down from the mast, a bat was snoring, fast asleep. "That's my airplane," said the Queen, who pointed at the bat and then chomped on her wing. The bat shrieked and fell, falling head first onto the crate's floor. "So, that's how you guard me now, is it?" shouted the Queen. "*That's* why I give you an entire slug at every meal?" A strong wave kicked up by a tourist boat sent us all tumbling to the bottom of the crate and we all took water up the nose; the mast gave way, fell into the water, and drifted quickly away. The bat took the accident quite philosophically, remarking: "We may have lost the mast, but we haven't lost the war," wiping the Queen's face with her wings as the latter sobbed and shouted: "Everyone's got it out for me, even the tourist boats!" Rakä and I slipped out of our soaked clothes and wrung them tight, hanging them to dry from the gangway rope while the Queen perseverated in her lamentation: "And as if that weren't enough, a human child dropped a fire truck into the villa!"

Rakä and I leaned over the crate's edge to watch a cappuccino-colored boy, about two years old with curly black hair and red overalls, try to stick his fat little hand into the willow roots to retrieve his plaything; from the other hole in the roots emerged a swarm of hamsters, stumbling over their shields; Iris and Carina (their dresses in tatters) climbed nimbly up onto the willow branches. Finally, the child started giggling, by which we understood that he'd managed to grab hold of his truck, but he immediately started crying, indicating that he was unable to remove his fist from the roots while still holding onto it. A female human with braids and a pale face approached him, taking him in her arms and cradling him, which only redoubled the child's sobs. "You're all worked up, my little rabbit," she said. "Where'd you put your big red fire truck?" The Queen, standing on the gangway rope, hollered orders to the stampeding army of hamsters (some climbed up onto the willow, while others threw themselves into the water and swam over to cling to the aircraft carrier). "Attack!" she cried, "rid me of these vandals!" And to the bat: "Go tangle yourself up in that human's hair," she commanded. But the bat pretended not to hear, busy as she was drying her wings in the breeze blowing in over the water. "With you as my witnesses," she said to Rakä and me, "I'm surrounded by poltroons!" The large human placed the small one in a stroller and began knitting a scarf, seated on a bench, telling him: "Until you behave, I won't let you out of there!" "We're saved!" the Queen exclaimed. "But for how long?" With her tail, she snatched an ice cream cone that was floating by on the Seine, bit a hole out of its tip, and used it as a megaphone, shouting: "In ninety seconds, a general staff meeting in the rat poison shelter on subfloor two; return in an orderly fashion and don't let me catch you lighting cigarette butts in the hall!" The hamsters went back in a jumble through the hole in the roots, though not without their share of gripes. The large human mother had fallen asleep on her knitting, a pair of jam jar bottoms hanging from the tip of her nose by iron wires, which were hooked over her ears.* Her little one tried to escape the stroller by swinging his arms like a windmill, with neither success nor despair. The bells of Notre-Dame rang seven o'clock, and all seemed rather calm on the Square du Vert-Galant, when a flock of sparrows swarmed the willow tree, chattering and shaking the branches, which

---

* Glasses. —Tr.

sent Iris and Carina tumbling down; they sneaked back over the gangway rope and climbed into the aircraft carrier crate. "There you are, at last!" the Queen said to them. "Ah, look at the state of your morning attire! I find that these two rats have been quite patient with you. Well then, you seem to be pregnant?" she snapped. The two sisters started crying, pointing at us with their tails. "Well, what dowry can you offer us?" the Queen asked. Rakä answered in a thin voice, "We own a six-egg polystyrene carton at the mouth of the sewer drain at the corner of Rue de Seine and Rue de Buci." "I'll take your word for it," said the Queen. "Do you love my daughters?" "Yes!" said Rakä. "But you look like nancy boys to me," said the Queen. "Only because of our outfits," said Rakä. "Which marionette shop do you buy your clothes at?" "The one on Rue Guénégaud," Rakä said, regaining a bit of his self-confidence while I continued trembling with fear. And after looking us over with the help of a contact lens she held up with the tip of her tail, she asked us, "Are you ready to take my daughters on as your cashiers?" "Yes," Rakä and I answered in unison. "And you, my daughters," she asked of her girls, "are you ready to leave the Île de la Cité to follow your husbands behind the counter?" Carina and Iris threw their forelegs around our necks, shrieking with joy and nibbling on our whiskers. The sparrows chirping in the willow tree plucked out leaves and let them fall over us. "Now here's an alliance that seems to please our allies the sparrows," the Queen said pensively, scratching her ear. Then, turning to her daughters, she said, "We may want to consider increasing the sparrows' share of seed! So, my sons," she said to us, patting us on the shoulders with her enormous paw, "are you happy now? You've just made the deal of a lifetime, believe me! My daughters are real gems, just like their mama!" And she burst out laughing. Then, turning to the bat: "Go squeeze me a grape, let's drink to this!" It started raining buckets. We all scurried back, crashing into each other along the gangway, to take shelter under the branches of the willow tree before the first bolt of lightning struck the spire of Sainte-Chapelle. The large human woke up, screamed, and grabbed the stroller with the child in it, coming to take shelter as well under the willow branches and nearly crushing us beneath her clogs. The hamster with the cider cap on his head approached, leaping over the puddles. "Everything's going wrong, Your Majesty! The forecast is calling for a storm on the Channel," he cried. "Raise the drawbridge," the Queen replied. "What drawbridge?" asked the army chief. "All of them!" she cried. The chief, deeply perplexed, retreated into the willow roots where the entire army was staying dry, and said: "All right, boys, time for a nap!" The troops, with a sigh of relief, disappeared underground.

"Members of the Court!" the Queen ordered, addressing Carina, Iris, Rakä, and me, plus the bat who was spreading her wings to serve as our umbrella. "Let's take shelter under the human's stroller!" We all ran under the baby stroller, where a strong scent of talc'd baby buttocks prevailed, warm and safe from the rain. The human mother was stomping her feet on the ground, crying out, "Damn rain!" and splashing mud on us with the heel of her clog, when suddenly we saw the child's fat hand appear under the stroller. The hand swiftly grabbed the Queen, who immediately vanished from sight. We, the Court, bounded onto the stroller's wheels; the Queen let out fearful little squeaks: the child had stuck her into his sweater and she was scrambling all around, unable to find an exit;

finally, she slipped into a sleeve where the child immobilized her, squeezing her tight in his other fist. The human mother screamed at him, "Are you going to stop squirming around in your stroller, you nasty little snot?" Overhead, the sun came back out and it stopped raining as if by magic. The human mother pushed the stroller back to the bench, which she dried with a Kleenex. We, the Court, climbed up the willow roots, trembling for the fate of the Queen, whom the child was still clutching in his sleeve as she gasped for air. Iris and Carina clung to our ears, sobbing. We soothed their jangled nerves with a couple of good slaps across the face as the bat had counseled, encouraging us on by saying: "It's what their dearly departed mother would have wanted." "Dearly departed?" Rakä shouted, regaining his Creole accent. "She's still alive!" "One rarely escapes from such situations," sobbed the bat, pointing her wing at the human mother as she gave her child his bottle and said: "Will you please sit still?" while the panicked Queen stuck her tail out of the sleeve in an attempt to escape. But the child held her tight in his fist. "I can't stand you today," the mother said, putting the child down on the ground. "Go and mind your own business, you little snot!" The child lumbered over our group on his stumpy hind legs, without letting go of the Queen imprisoned in his sleeve. From her basket, the mother produced a black radish, which she sliced on the knee of her jeans, and a Thermos of tea, with which she washed down the radish slices she crunched between her teeth, making an extremely unpleasant sound that was fortunately drowned out by the noise of traffic on the right bank of the Seine. The child plopped down onto his bottom and took the Queen out of his sleeve, dangling her by the tail in our faces. "Fiya twuck?" he asked, shaking the

Queen, who was trembling all over. "He wants his fire truck back in exchange for the Queen!" cried Rakä. "We'll have to rig up the car with a string! Calling all hamsters!" he shouted into the roots, "Emergency mission!" The hamsters scurried up, slipping back into their French Tickler collars. "But it's time for our nap," protested the hamster in the cider cap. "The Queen is in danger," shouted Rakä, dramatically accentuating his words. The hamsters raised their drowsy heads and saw the poor Queen hanging by her tail from the child's hand as he shook her ever harder, the better to flaunt his trophy. She lost her seal-wool wig and one shrimp shell boot, which the bat caught in her wings. "This is an emergency," the Queen said tremulously, upside down. "As soon as I'm free, we'll revisit that raise of yours!" The child pinned her mouth shut with his other hand and ran toward the human mother's bench, saying: "Glug, glug, glug!" "So now you want your bottle, you little snot," the mother said. "Take it and drink the whole thing by yourself!" The child took the bottle and went to hide under the bench, shaded from the sun, which had really started beating down after the rain cleared. He jammed the bottle's nipple into the Queen's mouth, nearly choking her, and forced her to drink half of its contents, which were shooting back out of her nostrils; we all recoiled in horror as the poor Queen turned green, on the verge of asphyxiation, and the child took evident pleasure in making her drink the boiling milk. Eventually, he yelled, threw the Queen and his bottle to the ground, and went to loll around in a puddle of rainwater near the willow roots. "You're an absolute monster today," the human mother said, picking up the bottle without noticing the Queen, who lay unconscious near the bench, and, turning on a transistor radio — its music occasionally interrupted by the time of day—went back to knitting a pair of red wool gloves. "And here I am, slaving away for you," she added distractedly to her son. "Will you stop rolling around in the mud already?" she insisted, before concentrating on the music, moving her knitting needles to its rhythm. Seeing that the coast was clear, we ran toward the Queen splayed out on the pavement, trailed by the hamsters who were heartened by Rakä's orders. We were amazed by and rather proud of the way Rakä kept his self-control* in such dire circumstances; without him, we surely would have panicked. The Queen continued vomiting curdled milk all over her beautiful onionskin coat. Rakä and I picked her up by the armpits and dragged her to the Seine, dipping her in the water while Iris and Carina rubbed her with toothpaste from a tube floating by near the bank. "Thank you, my sons," the Queen kept repeating. "What would have become of me without you?"

We were all about to get out of the water and go back to the willow roots when a shadow spread over us. The child was standing perfectly still on the riverbank, watching us. "Attack!" ordered the Queen. A heavy silence followed. Several hamsters hid their heads underwater and almost drowned, although the army chief gave a sign and threw a mustard lid against one of the child's shoes, shouting: "Hee, hee, hee!" as animals who stand erect tend to do when they want to frighten off creatures larger than themselves. The child fell back onto his buttocks and plunged his shoes into the water of the Seine, which caused a sort of whirlpool that

---

* This word appears in English in Gouri's original, but he certainly didn't learn it from me. —Tr.

knocked us off our feet. It was I who found myself thrust furthest from the shore by the force of a wave. I was swimming courageously toward the bank, watching the others scramble out of the water and bound into the willow branches, when I saw the shadow of the child's hand fall over me. I dove underwater, but his hand was quicker. A second later, I was already far from both water and terra firma, shivering with cold and fear in the closed fist of the child, who was staring straight at me.

The Human Child

EVERYONE ELSE, INCLUDING THE HAMSTERS, WAS shouting to me: "Stay strong! Stay strong!" from their perch in the willow branches. Then I saw the immense mouth of the child slowly open, revealing eight serrated incisors surrounded by four fangs. I steeled myself for the worst. The Queen and her daughters screamed in horror, and Rakä cried: "Bite his nose, Gouri!"* Suddenly, a pink tongue appeared from inside the mouth, quite thick as it emerged, then becoming pointy and thin the moment it touched my muzzle, which it licked before moving on to my whiskers and ears. Contact with this massive chunk of flesh disgusted me beyond all possible description. The tongue continued to lick my entire body. Even worse! It sucked my paws and tail. Then the child stuck my head in his mouth, and here I thought I was going to die of a heart attack: he squeezed my ribs with his teeth, all while pushing and pulling me in and out of his mouth. And the more this game amused him, the harder he sucked and bit down, pressing me so far into his throat that I thought he was going to swallow me alive. Finally, when I was fully inserted, he squeezed hard, holding me by the base of the tail. I began to struggle inside his mouth; his clenched teeth restrained

---

* It's curious that this is the only time the author's name appears throughout the tale. —Tr.

me. My position was made all the more uncomfortable by the fact that he was using the entire muscle of his tongue to pin me against his palate. Believing myself lost, I made one last effort to wheel around and bite his tongue, but it was so slippery that I couldn't sink my teeth in. And yet, in the end, this little merry-go-round of mine saved my life: By brushing his glottis with my whiskers, I made him vomit! His throat contracted, then he hurled a cyclone of goopy juice that swept me away. I was launched onto a cobblestone where I dislocated my tail and scraped my right ear badly, to say nothing of the state of my fur, which was soaked through with acidulated milk.

The human mother stepped away from her radio and knitting to come over to her son and say, "Did you throw up again? You're all worked up! What's gotten into you today, darling? Your shoes are soaked, you put your feet in the water! You little snot!" She slung the child over her elbow and went to change his shoes on the bench, which, miraculously, meant the coast was clear for now.

Rakä was the first to reach my side, clutching me in his arms, followed by the girls and the Queen; the hamsters, more prudent, stayed near the willow tree. "My brother!" cried Rakä. "Are you still with us?" I nodded. Carina nestled up to me, whimpering. The bat took me in her wings, and we all went back down into the willow roots, led by the hamsters who lit the corridor for us with torches carved out of matchsticks. The Queen took my pulse, proclaiming, "He's going to make it!" even though I was hardly wounded, just rather in shock from the danger I'd just escaped. "That I might die in my own bed..." I said to myself without much hope, for such is truly rare among rats. They set up a cot for me (a sponge in a sardine can) and laid me down in it, in the middle of the great hall, beside the fire truck. My wife Carina wiped me down as best she could with an already rather soiled sheet of newspaper, then rubbed me with scented honey to get the smell of vomit off me, before coquettishly combing my whiskers with an eyelash brush while the Queen and Rakä each held one of my hands. Such solicitude after my misadventure touched me deeply, and I began to weep with gratitude; the others comforted me with kind words.

But the calm didn't last long. The hamster chief came running in on all fours and cried, "The human chief is loose!" "To arms!" the Queen shouted at her soldiers, who were already fleeing into the villa's lower tunnels.

Out on the cobblestones, we heard the child's heavy footsteps as he approached the willow and gave the roots a good kick, sending a shiver down all our spines. Then all went silent. "The periscope!" cried the Queen. "Where the hell is my periscope?"

The Periscope

THIS PERISCOPE, WHICH THE HAMSTERS HAD FISHED up from the bed of the Seine, once belonged to a submarine. With great physical effort, we dragged it out of the cellars and set it up, lifting its eye through the willow roots and bracing the bottom against the fire truck, such that we could sit on the ladder and observe what was happening out on the Square du Vert-Galant. The child stood there motionless, staring at the roots, waiting, surely, for one of us to peek out so he could capture him. "Fortunately, there's no shortage of food to last us till nighttime," the Queen assured us, "and we can last several days if we grill up some hamsters!" I saw the hamster army chief's fur stand on end so high it lifted his cider-cap helmet. "But only in the case of urgency,"* added the Queen. "In the meantime, fetch us some olive pits to snack on during the state of siege," she ordered. The hamsters started frantically digging around for olive pits, when the Queen, standing on the ladder, cried: "Please don't panic! If we were even led, by dint of circumstance, to sacrifice you, you would be democratically selected at random, and I promise not to cheat in the lottery—Queen's word!" Then she invited the Court to sit on the ladder and look out through the periscope lens.

* Emergency. —Tr.

Rakä and I sat down beside our wives on the steps, and the bat took the driver's seat, only to fall asleep immediately on the steering wheel. The hamster chief climbed up next to me on the ladder, introducing himself with a salute. "Hamster chief want talk!" As I stood up to shake his hand, he removed his cider-cap helmet, and kissed my hand, whispering again, "Hamster want talk to Prince!"

"Silence on the ladder!" shouted the Queen, perched on the top step. The hamster chief, quivering with fear, nestled up to me on the ladder. It dawned on me then that Rakä and I had become princes by marrying the Queen's daughters. Carina, my wife, whispered in my other ear, "Watch out for that hamster, he's a conspirator!" Iris and Rakä nibbled on olive pits and drank from a brandied cherry on the rung above, all while following what was going on outside through the periscope. "Read this in due time, my Prince," said the hamster, slipping into my pocket a statement scrawled on a dead leaf. Then he scurried off on all fours into the lower tunnels, where the other hamsters had already taken refuge. I put my paw around Carina's shoulder while Rakä did the same with Iris, staring through the periscope lens. "That," said the Queen, pointing to the image, "is our common enemy, and he's playing the waiting game." The child was still staring at the root entrance, perfectly still. "And over there knitting," the Queen added, her mouth half-open, flashing her thick, gleaming, razor-sharp teeth, "is the despicable human mother." Her comments were made all the more superfluous by the fact that we could clearly see what was happening outside through the periscope, and nothing of note was taking place. I took the opportunity to read the hamster chief's statement. "Us want freedom. Signed: Hamsters and Moles."

"They're simply ridiculous," Carina told me, reading over my shoulder. "Mother grants them autonomy the first few days of every month, and they go spend their pay on mouselets of the night on Plateau Beaubourg, and, the very next day, they're back—with cases of gonorrhea that *we* have to treat. Not to mention the costs incurred by their clothing alone!" "But where are the moles?" I asked. "They escaped by digging a tunnel to Metro Cité. The fall of the house began when Daddy died," she whispered, plunging her snout deep in my ear. "Our mother manages our affairs haphazardly. Back when Daddy was still alive, we had a personal security force of huge Sicilian rats who forbade humans access to the Île de la Cité. But Mother ran out of money to pay them, so they ran off to join the police, and she replaced them with these hamsters." "I didn't realize the police had rats on payroll," I replied, surprised. "There's so much I don't know about the world," she intoned, stroking me with her tail. "How I'd love to learn it all." And, in a tinny voice, "If Mom didn't squander our inheritance at the casino, we'd be able to live the high life! Let's poison her!" I was taken aback. Rakä came to sit next to me, while Iris urinated on one of the fire truck's wheels and Carina chatted with her, powdering her whiskers with pepper.

"Gouri," Rakä whispered, "I don't like this at all." "I think they're just a little crazy," I said, "but not dangerous." "Oh, they're dangerous, alright," Rakä told me. "Look at how they treat the hamsters!" "But we're not hamsters!" I protested. "We will be soon if we don't get out of here. Those hamsters are just rats with their tails cut off!" he snapped. For a moment, I thought his abuse of brandied cherries had driven him mad. "Hamsters are all just tailless rats, everyone knows they're an inferior race," I retorted sharply. "Not these ones,"

Rakä said. I eyed a passing hamster, who was rolling a pine cone. And indeed, I noticed that his tail consisted of a single vertebra wrapped in a Band-Aid. My mustache stood on end, just like the day when I stuck my paw in your refrigerator's socket.

"Let's make a break for it, quick!" I exclaimed. "Yes, but how?" Rakä asked. "Even if we manage to sneak to the exit, the human child's waiting for us outside!" In any event, reaching the exit was unthinkable, given the number of hamsters bustling around us under the Queen's orders; three or four of them were tying a handkerchief to a drumstick to make a white flag they could wave from the opening in the roots. Others were painstakingly lifting a stone that had been swept into the kitchens during the downpour. Not to mention the dozens more who were busy bailing the water that had flooded said kitchens, working in a chain with the plastic wine caps they had previously used as helmets. The water, which they were unable to pour into the Seine due to the child's presence, ran a perfectly pointless course, because in the end it simply flowed down into the quarters of the Queen, who, mad with rage, ordered them to collect it once again and toss it into the subcellars where the hamsters barracked. The hamster chief, chastised, cleaned the salon's baseboards with his tongue, scrubbing the more stubborn stains with his whiskers sprinkled with dishwashing detergent.

Iris and Carina, meanwhile, were having fun whispering uproarious secrets into each other's ears and bathing in a cup of tea, lathering each other up with sugar and rubbing each other's backs with a spoon, while the hamsters fetched them clean clothes: kimonos cut out of tea napkins and slippers carved out of hazelnuts. They shouted at us: "Hey, hubbies, look how cute we look for you!" And they cackled like two screaming queens.

"See?" I said to Rakä. "These two girls really do love us, they would never even think of cutting off our tails!" "Keep a cool head," Rakä said. "Be especially wary of any narcotic they might slip into our food!" We were unable to discuss any further. The Queen approached us, climbing breathlessly up the ladder. "What hard work," she gasped, "being the Queen! They don't follow orders as fast as they did back in the days of my dear departed Raynaud, who had them under his thumb. I'll be counting on you, my sons, once you've learned our system!" "Technically, we were supposed to take your daughters on as cashiers at our humble little shop in the Buci market," Rakä said. "It was never a question of defending your willow tree against the humans, let alone leading the army of hamsters, who couldn't care less what's at stake!" ("Well put," I said to myself.) "I know, my son, but what do you want me to do about it? It is what it is! And to make matters worse," she said, weeping, "the bat — my beloved nurse — passed away in her sleep." The bat was indeed dead, smothered by her own wings on the fire truck's steering wheel. "Let's get her out of here before the rotten smell attracts the wasps! Get that corpse out of my salon!" she commanded the hamsters, who turned a deaf ear.

The Bat, the Fox Terrier, and the Bees

WE HELPED THE QUEEN ROLL THE BAT'S CORPSE INTO a ball and, pushing it with a stick, removed it from the willow roots. The human child lunged and grabbed her in his fist; as soon as he realized the bat wasn't moving anymore, his eyes opened wide, he ran over to his mother, who was still knitting, and he laid the bat's corpse on her knee. The mother let out a long, sustained scream on the bench, then jumped onto the cobblestones to give the child a slap so hard that we all leapt to the periscope to get a better look. Once his shock had worn off, the child started screaming even louder than his mother had; she shook him like a rag doll and dragged him over to the Seine, washing his hands and yelling: "Don't put your fingers in your mouth or I'll kill you," her yellowish-blue eyes bulging out of their sockets. Then she stuck the child back in his stroller; he kept on screaming, pausing from time to time to catch his breath, while she pushed the bat with the toe of her clog all the way to the Seine, where her corpse drifted away with outspread wings. "Will you be quiet, you little snot?" the mother shouted at the child, who could hardly hear her over his own screams. "We're saved," we all sighed in the roots, "but for how long?" The mother's behavior was quite erratic, now she punished the child by imprisoning him in his stroller, now she smothered him with kisses and set him free to come torment us. "Let's take this chance to sneak over there and tie the child to his stroller," Rakä proposed. But the enterprise, however heroic, struck us as impracticable.

Even so, we all climbed out of the roots (even the hamsters) to make the most of the truce and loll about in the last puddles of warm water on the cobblestones. We were rubbing each other to work our courage back up, when a little white fox terrier, about three months old and wearing a waxed tartan raincoat, came bounding down the steps of the Henri IV statue before it leapt at us, barking hysterically and blocking the entrance to the roots. We quickly escaped into the willow branches. The Square du Vert-Galant was suddenly filled with humans and dogs of all ages and races, which made our situation even more difficult. The child, after crying in his stroller for fifteen minutes straight, fell into a deep sleep. The fox terrier, on the other hand, upheld his siege without fail or reprieve for two full hours. He ran around the tree, pissing in every entrance to the roots, then barked, staring us down and uttering threats that gave us such shivers that we had to clutch the branches with all our limbs to keep from falling. What's more, we suffered several minor attacks from all sorts of other beasts. A seagull came out of nowhere and pecked at the Queen before it relieved her of her shrimp shell boots and flew away. The sun was beating down and we had nothing to drink, so we chewed the willow's leaves to freshen our buccal mucosae. The heat attracted a swarm of bees that lived on Île Saint-Louis, which drove their stingers savagely into our buttocks before stealing off with drops of willow nectar. The fox terrier's owner (a human with dentures and white hair that made him look like a rabbit, dressed entirely in white save his Rolex), finally had the good sense to put the dog on a leash and tie it to the back of the bench, where he then sat and opened a book beside the human mother who was listening to her radio, connected to her ear by an electric wire. The human child was finally awakened by the whining of the dog, who was on the verge of strangling himself with his collar, unable to coordinate his simultaneous impulses of fight and flight. The child woke up yawning and looked around sleepily, then, his gaze growing increasingly keen, he inspected the changes of scenery and the locations of living beings and their behavior. (Here a passage follows which I found prudent to elide, since the author goes on and on with descriptions of the behavior of dogs and humans that are extremely tedious for us because they're common knowledge; I also cut a long conversation between the child's mother and the dog's owner concerning frozen food products. Meanwhile, the Rat Court and Hamster Brigade managed to reach the willow roots, where they painstakingly hoisted the toy fire truck out of their lair. I resume the narrative without further omissions.)

The human child, freed from his stroller, jumped on the white fox terrier in the tartan raincoat, who was tied to the bench, and nearly strangled him, yanking on the dog's leash and pinning its neck with his heel against the cobblestones. The dog's owner, the homosexual dressed in white with a gold Rolex on his wrist and an old leather-bound literary volume in hand (which he tossed aside), rushed over to separate them — as did the child's mother, who dropped her knitting, her radio, and her Thermos. The dog whimpered as he licked the shoes of the homosexual, who picked him up to comfort him, while the human mother reprimanded the human child and shook him by the arm. But permit me this aside so I can tell you about the situation we rats found ourselves in just then. Once the coast was clear for us to reach the willow roots, the hamster chief and the Queen of Rats made a pact, after lengthy discussion, that the hamsters would carry the fire truck up from the bottom of the roots to the cobblestone surface in exchange for a four-day weekend, which they would spend on the right bank, on the other side of the Pont-Neuf where, it seems, a number of their cousins lodge in a shop. Once the truck had been removed, we thought of giving it back to the child, in hopes that such a gesture would bring us peace. Now that the child was back in his stroller and the fox terrier was tied back up to the bench, the mother returned to her radio, the homosexual to his Racine, the hamsters, ever fearful, refused to push the truck toward the bench, claiming that their long weekend had already begun. They each took a backpack filled with seeds and went whistling off in single file along the water's edge, pledging to return in four days' time. We, the Court, resolved to push the fire truck over to the child, taking advantage of both the large humans' distracted state and the little human and fox terrier's immobility. The Queen got in behind the wheel. Iris, Carina, Rakä, and I were pushing the truck when the homosexual suddenly looked up from his book and was, at first, no doubt, surprised to see the fire truck moving by itself, then, spotting us, howled and hopped up onto the bench. The mother immediately did the same; as for the fox terrier, he barked his head off. The child was the only one who didn't lose his cool, he rocked in the stroller until it fell to the ground, scampering out at top speed and running toward us on his stumpy legs. "All hands to the aircraft carrier!" Rakä ordered, now that our path to the willow tree had been cut off by the child. We rushed onto the carrier, counting on the child to stop and retrieve his fire truck, but he did nothing of the sort; he stalked us, the Court, letting out little giggles: "Hee! Hee! Hee!" I realized in a flash that he was trying to imitate our language. The mother let out sustained howls that betrayed her Germanic origins (later on we learned that the child was the fruit of a furtive union between her and a Senegalese student in the hallways of the Alliance Française), as for the homosexual, he was the first to regain his composure and step down from the bench to unleash his fox terrier, who lunged at us as fast as a race car as he passed the child. All the while, we, the Court, were frantically gnawing at the rope attaching the willow roots to the vegetable crate (which, by some extreme aberration, we continued referring to as "the aircraft carrier"), Rakä, who had stayed behind on the bank (about a foot away), pounced to bite the dog's snout, all while dodging his admittedly deft fangs. The fox howled in retreat. As he attacked again, the human child popped up behind him, closed two hands around his throat and, lifting him into the air, swung him around before bashing his head against the tree trunk, just as the homosexual rushed over to snatch him out of the child's hands. This incident bought us some time: the aircraft carrier was hanging on now by only a few strands of rope. The Queen and her daughters got busy gnawing at them as I leapt to Rakä's rescue; he was holding his own against the human mother, who, in the meantime, had rushed over with her stroller to try and crush him. All of a sudden, the rope snapped apart. We all jumped into the water, clinging to the aircraft carrier as it was swept away in the current, just as the human child dropped his whole bottom onto us. The carrier plunged underwater and nearly flipped over, before it floated back up. We all jumped onto the child, who had gotten stuck in the aircraft carrier (as before in the stroller) and Rakä and I grabbed hold of his hair, while our stepmother the Queen and our two wives Iris and Carina crawled into his socks so as not to be taken under by the waves. The human mother, however, threw herself at us headfirst, tripping over her stroller, bashing her head on a paving stone, and falling into the water, bleeding hard from her forehead. The homosexual ran into the water to grab her by the hair, but he lost his footing, while the aircraft carrier floated off in circles toward the Académie Française, far to the left of the Pont des Arts, and the homosexual, who didn't know how to swim, clung to the human mother, who, in turn, clung to him, howling and gurgling. The fox terrier swam around them, barking, and scrambled up onto their heads, which soon disappeared in a whirlpool, leaving only the dog, who paddled back to the right bank, shaking himself off in his tartan raincoat before relieving himself on a post and vanishing from sight, heading back up the stairs that lead to the Jardin des Tuileries.

Vidvn

OUR CRATE SAILED SWEETLY ALONG THE LEFT BANK. THE Queen of Rats and her two daughters, the princesses, stretched out on the child's chest to dry off in the sun while Rakä went diving in the Seine (I held him by the tail, hooking my own to the crate) to fish up a sturdy stem to use as an oar, with which he managed to steer clear of a swirling current that threatened to send us crashing into a floating pool for humans that was tied to the bank. The café au lait–colored child, practically wedged in the crate, understood our intentions and used his arms as propellers to return us to the middle of the Seine where, beyond the Pont de la Concorde, we could glide in certain currents the Queen of Rats claimed to know well, and be swept under the Pont Alexandre-III, after which we could run the crate aground in an outcropping of rushes and easily reach the shore upon the child's shoulders. Just then, however, we saw the approach of one of those enormous four-decker tourist boats encased in plexiglass, on which swarms of Asian tourists make their rounds of the islands on the Seine before rushing under Place de la Concorde to visit the sewers. Several hundred of them, seeing the red of the child's overalls, photographed us as our crate was drawn inexorably closer to the boat's bow; we quickly abandoned the crate and clung to the child's hair as he sank, holding his breath underwater, which allowed us to narrowly escape the boat's metal propeller as the flock of Asian tourists ran up and down the deck, photographing us all the while. The boat cruised off toward the Île de la Cité. The child, exhausted, simply let himself float for a moment, then slowly started to back-paddle toward the left bank, under the Pont Alexandre-III, aided by the current and the counsel of the Queen, who was clinging to his ear and shouting by turns: "On board! To port! To starboard!" while we, the Court, clung to his overalls. At last, he reached the bank, short of breath; during the final few yards, we had to throw ourselves into the water and tug on his straps with our teeth while he floated on his back. Once his buttocks were on solid ground, he burst into laughter and started clapping. We, the rats, did the same, kissing each other's whiskers and squeaking with joy. The child picked us up and threw us into the air, catching us only to throw us up again, which gave us a reassuring jolt of vertigo. After this, we could tell he really loved us. Seeing him shivering in his cold, soaked clothing, we undressed him with great difficulty; the water had shrunk his overalls' buttonholes so much that the buttons no longer fit through, and we had to nip them off with our teeth.

That was when we realized this child was not a male, as we had believed up to this point, but a female, still hairless on her pubis and not deflowered, about two years old, which, while young for a human, represents (if one adjusts for time zones and cellular aging, as I recently read in a scientific journal) about one week in the life of a rat; so we decided to treat her like a child of our own. She was wearing a chain bracelet around her wrist with the name AIDAN, or rather ∀ID∀И,*

---

* Knowing how rats invert their script, I deduced that the little girl's name must have been Nadia. —Tr.

on it. She rolled around on the ground giggling when we tickled her feet and ribs. We laid her overalls out in the sun, washed her urine- and excrement-soaked diapers in the Seine, scrubbing them with our whiskers, while Vidvn* sucked down a half-full tin can of good corned beef crawling with maggots. Then we, the Court in exile, held a summit around a makeshift table on a brick. The Queen was in favor of blockading both entrances to the Pont Alexandre-III bridge and confronting the humans, holding the child as our hostage, demanding that the human authorities send a helicopter to transport us back to our Île de la Cité—a plan we all resolutely opposed (we didn't even have the backing of the Hamster Brigade, presently on leave).

Walking back to the Square du Vert-Galant would have been foolish at a time when so many humans were strolling along the banks of the Seine; our only course of action was to wait for nightfall. We all agreed, despite a certain reluctance on the part of the Queen, who would have liked to declare all-out war on the police. Vidvn, having lost the thread of our discussions, fell asleep, sucking her thumb. We rolled her into a hollow at the foot of the bridge that smelled strongly of human urine, making it a perfect place to sleep, and covered her with some rags we found lying around. We were very tired and decided to take a nap while awaiting the distant nightfall; it was hardly eleven o'clock in the morning and crowds of Parisian women were invading the banks of the Seine with their dogs, spouses, children, and parents; thankfully, our den was practically invisible to such people, who get out to the banks of the Seine but one spring afternoon per year and, so

---

* The human child will be called Vidvn for the rest of the story. —Tr.

bemused by the scenery and probably unaware of the existence of rats, hardly bother to look into holes in the ground. Vidvn snuggled up in the den and we in her armpits to stay warm before we all fell into a deep sleep, after a brief prayer to the Rat God.

Mimile

I WOKE UP AS THE SUN WAS GOING DOWN, AND THE ONLY sounds were the streaming water and a few distant cars on the right bank. Rakä was shaking my shoulder and motioning for me to keep quiet. A female human was standing in front of us, staring us down, completely still. She was of indeterminate age, though surely very old; in any event, the skin on her face was as shriveled as a desiccated bladder, with plenty of soot in its wrinkles, her white hair filthy and in disarray, only three yellow teeth behind her lips. She was wearing a torn bure dress and a blanket with holes at her shoulders, two nearly black basketball socks rolled up above her slippers, her two hands clutching a plastic wine bottle, from which she took a hearty swig before she continued to eye us. Behind her stood a rather stocky man who leaned on a large baby stroller of the old-fashioned sort* with a collapsed wicker chair inside it. The man was very hairy and, even from afar, smelled like a goat; he was wearing a long black overcoat with a missing back flap over a pair of blue jeans that didn't quite reach the tops of his foreign legion boots, a red cravat tied around his neck, no shirt, and a crumpled panama hat. "Lookee here, Mimile, we've got a visitor," the woman said.

---

* A landau-style baby carriage, I imagine. —Tr.

"Somebody tucked this little black rugrat up in our hole, I can't believe it! Plus, she's in her birthday suit!" "That's not true," said Mimile. "You're just seeing things again, Berthe." "I swear on my mama's head," said Berthe. "There's even a little brood of rats traipsing round on her." Mimile let go of the stroller to walk over to us; we didn't think of scattering, having ascertained, from his leisurely process of thought, that the man wasn't a danger. They both sized us up for a while until Vidvn woke up, squealing. We rats tried to calm her down, nestling against her cheeks. "She's hungry," said the Queen of Rats. And she shouted at the human woman, "Couldn't you breastfeed her instead of standing around and gawking at us like a fool?" The humans' jaws dropped when they heard the Queen speak. "Those rats can talk!" the female cried. "Kick 'em out, Mimile, this is our hole!" "But what'll we do about the girl?" asked Mimile. "Chuck her in the Seine! Last thing we need's a kid!" "No, no!" cried the Queen of Rats. "The child is ours! I'm the Queen of Rats and she is our hostage!" "Oh, now I've heard it all!" said the female. "If you're the Queen of Rats, then I'm the Queen of Humans!" "So be it," said the Queen of Rats. "This is my Court, allow me to introduce you to my twins, the princesses Iris and Carina, and my two sons-in-law, my heirs apparent, Gouri and Rakä." We all bowed reverentially while the Queen of Humans burst out laughing. She took a swig from her bottle before spitting the ammonic wine in our faces. Vidvn started to cry and Mimile took her in his arms, rocking her back and forth. "Don't you dare touch the kid," cried the Queen of Humans, shaking him. "You're jealous," said Mimile. Without letting go of Vidvn, he socked the Queen of Humans in the face, and she rolled around on the ground without letting go of her bottle. He emptied the stroller of the wicker chair, a crate full of rotten vegetables, and a heater, then he sat Vidvn down inside it, handing her an old cauliflower to nibble on. The Queen of Humans struggled to her feet, crying, "Police! Police!" Then she hit Mimile on the head with her plastic bottle, shouting, "I pulled you out of the river, and this is how you thank me? I'll kill that little brat!" And she sprang at Vidvn, intending to strangle her. Mimile picked up a rock and bashed the Queen of Humans' head until blood flooded her white hair and she was rolling around on the ground. Vidvn leaned out of the stroller to get a better look; as for us rats, we kept our distance. Mimile took a large knife out of the stroller and sank it into the neck of the Queen of Humans, who moaned and jolted, then lay still; he dragged her by the hair to the Seine and kicked her in; she drifted away. Mimile spat on the water, unbuttoned his fly, and urinated at length. Then, approaching Vidvn in the stroller, he picked her up and gave her a big hug. She went right along with it, completely happy; we could tell he was a friend, then, and we approached the group. Mimile licked Vidvn's whole body with his big tongue, which made her laugh, tickled by his beard. Then he dressed her in a navy blue sweater that hung down to her knees and stashed the red overalls in a hole he covered with dirt before pulling out a bone, which he gave to us and on which we, the Court, nibbled out of politesse, even though our religion forbids us from consuming beef. He told us, "You've got nothing to fear from me, my rats, I also know what life is like." Then, sitting down on the broken wicker chair, he took Vidvn in his arms, gave her some wine to drink from a bottle, and said, "Would you all like to hear the story of my life?" We all answered "yes" in unison and went to sit in a circle around him. Apart from you, Master, this was the only human in my entire existence who ever addressed either me or the Court; we were moved to tears, a fact the Queen conveyed in a brief speech of gratitude. We were keenly interested in what a human's life might be like, and we all opened our ears wide, except Vidvn, who was busy suckling Mimile's chest hair and beard instead of listening to his speech. "I," said Mimile, "have no memory. Whenever they toss me in the clink, I can't remember what for; that's my bad luck. Last time, seems like I killed some old man while I was robbing him, time before that it was a toddler, and I'd raped him. It always turns out the same way: they lock me up and shave my head, but I'm slippery; just last week, I bumped off the nurse at Clairvaux and sneaked out in her scrubs, but I'll probably forget that one soon, too. My specialists say I have no memory because I took shrapnel in the skull back in the Legion, but that's not right, I never took any shrapnel, that's the only thing I *do* remember." Then he fell silent. We rats were a bit disappointed by the gaps in his story, but it stood to reason that humans should have virtually no memory, seeing how many of them devote their lives to writing, painting, sculpting, photographing, and recording their voices, their deeds and attitudes, whereas if we had no memory, our species would inevitably go extinct. The Queen was of the opinion that humans would vanish from the surface of the earth once they had fully reproduced themselves in objects, which we rats would keep as souvenirs, as happened to so many beasts of the Tertiary period, of which we have only molds now; Rakä, ever the optimist, stated his hope that humans might survive as long as rats; given the torpor their lack of memory brings about, I seriously doubt it. Mimile had already forgotten about us and was crying, hugging Vidvn, and saying, "You're the only thing I've got in this world, kid, don't leave me." We used this opportunity to bid farewell, seeing that Vidvn was in good hands, and attempt to make it back to the Île de la Cité before dark; we were preparing to walk up the Seine's left bank, when a big black cat with a reddish spot on its muzzle jumped us. We all panicked and took refuge on Vidvn and Mimile; he grabbed the cat by the scruff of the neck and stuck it in a woman's handbag, which he closed over the cat and punted into the Seine while Vidvn giggled with delight. Such kindness from a human being struck us as divine in nature, and we wondered if Mimile wasn't the eternal man who, in the religion of rats, descends from the sky but once every ten thousand years to rid the earth of the cats who, unfortunately, until now, have always risen from their ashes. Our presumption was practically confirmed by a phrase of Mimile's when he booted the bagged-up cat into the Seine: "One Mimile makes two *mille* in the year ten *mille*!" he said, threatening the sky with his fist, then burst out laughing and swigged down the rest of his bottle of Préfontaines before taking his sex out of his fly and wagging it around, offering it to Vidvn, who began to suckle it hungrily. Until this point, we had never known that the human male's penis serves the same function as the female's udder, and perhaps even more effectively, since the pleasure they derive from it is more intense and the form of the male penis better suited to the shape of the human mouth once the gums have grown teeth, although the milk does take longer to come out of the male than the female, and it emerges in spurts, as we observed from up close. Perhaps I'm boring you, dear Master, with these observations which, while surprising to us rats, are surely commonplace to you, but, you must understand, I write everything I see. That's how your favorite English authors write, the ones you used to read to me in my already distant childhood. Since I last saw you, plenty of water has flowed under the bridges of the Seine, I married the princess Carina and we're expecting a litter, my life is "normal," so to speak, even though I don't love my wife and I prefer practically anyone else in the world to her, that's just how the cookie crumbles. The others have fallen asleep, so I'm taking the opportunity to finish this letter on a sheet of the *France-Soir* with which Mimile wiped his anus, his leftover excrement serving as ink in which I dip the tip of a matchstick, by the light of a candle stub, hoping to find a stamp to post it off one of these days. Vidvn, as soon as she swallowed Mimile's milk, fell fast asleep on the ground between his legs, with his penis in her mouth. Mimile snores loudly, to keep the cats away; the Rat Court has settled down, curled in a ball in a coat inside the stroller; as for me, I'm writing by the riverbank, sitting on a cobblestone. I yawn, a cool breeze brings a new morning. I kiss you four times on your two cheeks, Master. I'm going to curl up, to sleep with my kind. Til soon. Your Gouri.

The Capture

DEAR MASTER, I'LL PICK UP WHERE I LEFT OFF. AFTER giving Vidvn and Mimile a kiss goodnight, I curled into a ball with the rats of the Court, and we all held each other tight. The Queen of Rats, in her sleep, kept repeating, "Shamed be whomever Mimile pisses on." Rakä and I shook her by the ears to wake her up but she only switched nightmares, squealing, "Give them cake! Give them cake!" It was unbearable; both of our wives complained that they couldn't sleep, which would have serious repercussions on the nervous systems of Rakä's and my respective litters, and they demanded that we push their mother out of the stroller* so as not to have to hear her anymore. Rakä threw a fit, telling them quite rightly that their mother's nightmares bothered us less than their gripes; I agreed and we got out of the stroller to go nestle up in one of Mimile's shoes. We fell asleep there, Rakä and I, in a tender embrace, swearing that we would never set foot in the Rat Court again, and that at first light we would return to our little shop on Rue de Buci, as we found our wives' attitudes intolerable, going so far as to even contemplate divorce so we could get back to business together. Mimile rolled over in his sleep and expulsed a great gust of sulfurous wind from his

---

* The carriage. Rats confuse strollers and carriages. —Tr.

anus while embracing Vidvn, who was suckling his nose. We took advantage of their movements to slip in between their warm bellies: it was cold out. Our two wives and their mother, the Queen of Rats, argued in the carriage, crying and biting each other over matters of inheritance. Rakä and I turned a deaf ear and fell back asleep, whisker to whisker.

I dreamed that I was myself, but that my tail ended in the head of a cat who was trying to nip my snout, and I spun in faster and faster circles to escape him. Then an enormous eagle-headed seagull swallowed the cat's head before dissolving, making way for a sphinx with Rakä's body and Mimile's head; it slowly undulated its hips, and from its tail a red spider dangled on a thread, which woke me with a start. I clung to Rakä with all four legs to fall back asleep when I saw, on the inside of my eyelids, a fireball that turned blue until it exploded, giving rise to a multitude of white saucers on which green iguanas spun like tops, then I dreamed of nothing until I saw a purple dinosaur swallow the sphinx, spread its wings — quite similar to the bat's, and turning yellow — and smile kindly at me before fading into the void, which allowed me to fall into a much-needed restorative but, alas, short-lived sleep. I was cozy and warm in the crook of Mimile's scrotum when a bright light awoke me. A score of human police officers were standing in a circle around our group, pointing searchlights at us. Rakä and I jumped quickly into the stroller to hide out with the Queen of Rats and her two daughters. Just then, Mimile was awakened by Vidvn's sobs, who was squealing as only she knows how, and clinging to his neck. Mimile wrapped one arm around her and was reaching for his knife with the other when the cops jumped him. They tore Vidvn out of his grasp before rolling him over on the ground; two of them kicked him in the kidneys and gut while another clubbed his head; a fourth quickly cuffed his wrists behind his back. A man dressed like a Chicago mobster headed the operation, barking curt orders. "Pardieu and Donadieu, take the little girl to the Hôtel-Dieu, have them check to see if she was raped, then meet me at the Prefecture. We'll take the rats in this carriage as evidence!" A riot shield fell over the stroller, forming a lid and leaving us no way out; we all huddled together, terrified, in the dark. Vidvn kept on crying while they carried her away; Mimile must have fainted or been so stunned by the blows that he remained silent. "Emile Canard," cried the pig, "this time, it's off with your head!" "But my name's not Canard—it's Rouge-Gorge!" Mimile said, breathlessly, then he yelled "ouch" before falling quiet. "You know perfectly well that you killed the cultural attaché to Senegal's wife to kidnap his daughter. You scumbag! And not even a week has passed since you escaped Clairvaux by slaughtering a nurse!" "I don't remember a thing," said Mimile. "You never remember a thing," said the cop, "but it'll all come back to you when your neck's under the guillotine, Emile Canard!" By Mimile's groans, we could tell they were manhandling him. We rats, however frightened we may have been, knocked on the shield with our tails to let them know that we had witnessed the perfectly accidental death of Vidvn's mother, but a cop smacked the carriage cover with his billy club, stunning us, and we fell silent. The stroller was wheeled brutally into a paddy wagon along with the gasping Mimile, and then . . .

(Translator's note: I'll allow myself a parenthetical here for the reader's sake: Mimile was not named Emile Canard but Emilio Draconi, and he was beheaded at Fresnes Prison

53

in August 1978; I received these letters two months prior. I ran to show them to my editor, who called me insane. Emilio Draconi was sentenced to death for the murders of Madame Koulobô (Vidvn's mother) and Bianco Cazzo di Fiori, the homosexual in white from the beginning of this story. Yet the letters you are reading are clear proof of his innocence. Of all the misdeeds this man in fact committed (if I'm to trust the papers, he began at ten by strangling his mother to make off with her divorce settlement), he was sentenced to death for the accidental deaths of these two ridiculous characters who threw themselves into the Seine in pursuit of rats, when they didn't even know how to swim. As for the murder of Berthe the tramp—the one Gouri calls the Queen of Humans—that one was pinned on another hobo named Bébert, who had been seen trying to strangle her on Place de la Contrescarpe shortly beforehand. I won't recount all of my efforts, but I will say that I managed, thanks to my publisher, to get an appointment with the Minister of the Interior, though nobody chose to believe the authenticity of these letters. I was able to send Mimile one pack of cigarettes per day and a handful of detective novels, and I was present, by special favor of his lawyer, at his execution. He was a swart fellow, rather plain and maybe even a bit slow. Although he was aware of his fate, he did not stand up to his executioners with the verve that Gouri's narration grants him, paralyzed either by fear or by medication. Now that I've conveyed to you the spectacle's grimmer details, I'll cede the floor once again to the Rat, who is better informed about the matters at hand.)

The Snake

BONJOUR, MASTER: THINGS ARE GOING TERRIBLY, FOR me and the Rat Court. They locked us up in a cage in the basement of the Prefecture of Human Police; there were other pieces of evidence in the cages around us, too: the poodle of a Vietnamese streetwalker who got hacked to pieces by a Moroccan man, the snake of a belly dancer disemboweled by a Belgian redhead, and the same white fox terrier from this morning, suspected of rabies, whose tartan raincoat had been confiscated. The fox terrier and poodle were barking all sorts of madness at each other; as for the snake, he was snoring, rolled up at the bottom of his cage. "You're in luck," he said through the bars, suddenly waking up. "As for us, they're going to cut off our heads, which can't just be stuck back on. But you, they'll send you over to the human lab, where you might be able to escape if you play dead." Hearing this, the thick fur on our tense bodies stood straight up. We'd heard stories about human laboratories, how they pierce the skin with metal instruments flowing with electricity or poisonous liquids, to study the rats' behavior in the face of death and draw psychological conclusions that facilitate their work in human prisons and camps, but we hardly believed them, assuming they were just macabre tall tales. The snake hissed at the dogs, who fell silent, trembling with fear in their respective cages, and continued in this manner: "As a snake,

I could slip through the bars and out of my cage, since that's how we were built; but I'm not interested in escape; in here, I'm kept cool and well fed, they give me one nice rat per day, but in your case they give you only dog food, which is of far worse quality." This was indeed a serpentine speech, typical of a snake pretending to be your friend while awaiting his chance to swallow you whole, but one point was plain and the Queen of Rats seized on it immediately: "Let's make a pact against the humans," she proposed to the snake. The snake opened his eyes wide and raised his head to listen more closely. "I've always dreamed of swallowing a fat, clean-shaven human whole," he said, "but I never dared dream it might be possible." "Haven't you heard of pythons?" said the Queen. "Are those the ones that are as long as this hallway and wider than this column, the ones that live in the Amazon?" asked the snake. "I was born in the Sahara, and down there we're all small and muscular so we can hide in the sand and pop back out." While the Queen of Rats described the Amazon to the astonished serpent, Rakä and I made an agreement: rather than allowing ourselves to be sent to a human lab, we would carry out a suicide pact. We didn't breathe a word of this to our wives, who were quite oblivious to the situation (most likely trusting in our absolute power, despite all evidence to the contrary), busy sweeping our cage with their tails (a rather filthy cage, I should mention, as its previous occupant was a molting green parrot, witness to the assassination of a Russian princess). While they cleaned, they came up with all sorts of names for the pinkies of our respective litters, even though it wasn't at all certain they would see the light of day—we chose not to worry them. We were bothered to no end by the fox terrier, who peed on us through the bars, and the whining of the poodle, who was clearly the only one who gave us no cause for worry, the Human Society for Animals makes sure to place purebred dogs with purebred people, where they always keep bones on hand and grooming is compulsory, which is what gives them that ridiculous appearance; in any event, they're better off than we are. The Queen of Rats, seeking to gain the snake's complicity, praised the golden-brown color of his skin; the snake contorted with delight, flattered by the praise but trying not to show it: "Oh, these little things? They're just prison tattoos, you could get some, too, if you shaved. Of course, they look prettier on me because I don't have any limbs, but you could conceal yours by hiding them under your ears." The Queen offered the excuse that her job as Queen forced her to use her ears and paws so she could listen and give orders, to which the snake replied: "To each her kingdom, my dear." That one really got the dogs in their cages laughing. Our guard, sitting next to us, woke up and smacked the bars with his billy club. We all went silent and still, waiting for him to fall back asleep and start snoring, then spoke more quietly: "We snakes, my children," the snake said, having captured the attention of his audience by his position in the central cage, "enjoy an advantage over you quadrupeds in that we don't have limbs, which weigh down the gait; it also ensures increased circulation to the brain, which proves our superior intelligence." And he gave a demonstration, lowering his head and spinning his tail like a lasso. We all expressed our sincere admiration and the Queen of Rats even invited him to spend his Easter vacation curled up in our tree, should he, the tree, and we ourselves be alive and free from captivity come Easter. The poodle and the fox terrier, tired of acting like dogs, joined us to confess that they were also captives (in their condition as canines); at first, dogs had joined forces with humans by giving up their tails and ears, which the famished Andean Indians tribes ate in exchange for human excrement (which dogs are still crazy for, but which they are now forbidden), then, as hunger became more pressing, they had no choice but to take on menial human tasks, as we all know, a point we all agreed—snakes and rats alike—was worthy of our disdain. They lowered their ears and wept, but tough luck. "This is no time to take pity on each other just because we happen to be prisoners in neighboring cages," said Rakä, and the dogs swore to us that, even outside, they would stand united with us against the humans. The discussion became interminable. First, our wives Iris and Carina wanted to expound on their condition as females in the face of the males of all species, to which the snake replied that he was a hermaphrodite and that, in fact, he impregnated himself by inserting his head into his only orifice, which stupefied me, however natural the others found it, or at least pretended to. In short, the snake promised never to eat another rat again, the poodle that he would never obey another human command, the fox terrier that, from now on, he would come and live a fox's life with us in the willow roots, and the poodle one-upped him, swearing that he would go off to live as a hermit in the desert, dressed in a white tunic. And with these fine words, we all fell asleep, dreaming of our unlikely, if not impossible, freedom, when . . .

The Pieces of Evidence

... WHEN A MAN'S HAND CAME DOWN ON OUR CAGE, lifted us up, and threw us into a cart, which another man pushed on creaky wheels down a hallway and into an electric elevator, while the snake, poodle, and fox terrier whistled and barked to wish us good luck. The elevator stopped on the floor above and in came Mimile, being held up by others, his face as swollen as a mandrill's ass. When he saw us, he cried, "My rats! Victory is ours!" and we gave him a heartily greeting, bounding around inside our cage. The elevator stopped again and opened on a square-shouldered woman in a shoddy, whitish guanaco wig, a black tunic fit for a priest, only in lighter fabric, over a plain gray Chanel suit and a gray-on-gray striped scarf by Grès (the tags, still attached, were visible), her legs sheathed in plain beige stockings and black crocodile pumps. Her facial expression made her look a bit like Vidvn's mother, only in deeper absentia,* with a bit more color around her two nostrils, which reminded me of our Frigidaire's socket, master. Under her right arm, she was holding several pounds of paper cut into rectangles, holding it tight so as not to drop it. The elevator opened once again at the floor above and an

---

* Some of Gouri's expressions remain foreign to me, but I have maintained them as they appear; maybe the reader will understand them more clearly than I do. —Tr.

extremely tall and fat policewoman came in, holding Vidvn in her arms. When Vidvn saw Mimile, she sobbed with joy and asked to leave with him. Mimile started to shout: "My girl! My girl!" They beat him back, Vidvn began to cry, and we all shouted "Bonjour!" from our cages. When the door opened again, we all ran out into a long hallway and moved very quickly between two streams of people who were busy running around and talking to each other, some dressed like the woman in the elevator, in a white wig and black tunic, but with pants instead of skirts. The Queen explained to Rakä and me: "Those are lawyers — *avocats*, in French; they get their name from the words *abacaxi* and *ahogado*, which mean *pineapple* and *drowned* in Portuguese and Spanish, respectively. A simple folk," she added, "their work consists in arguing either for or against people who have been accused of crimes before a jury made up of their mothers, and the verdict is pronounced by their fathers." "The parents of the accused?" I asked, reasoning that Mimile's mother and father would never condemn him (to death, at least). A likely story! "The mothers and fathers of the lawyers," the Queen retorted. Seeing as the lawyers' mothers and fathers were also dressed like the lawyers and differed only in the quantity of wrinkles on their faces, we got them all confused before they had even taken their place behind the counters of a square room, the fathers to the right, the mothers to the left, and the lawyers circulating in the middle, shouting loudly and pointing at us, the pieces of evidence, as proof of Mimile's degree of malice and degradation; they referred to him as Emile Dragon, and when the lawyers argued amongst themselves, the fattest among them, who was seated at the center (he must have been their common grandfather), pounded on his table with a hammer, pretending to nail it back together, which silenced the others as they plugged their ears. We understood that the source of their disagreement was the price of Mimile's head; it seemed to us the height of absurdity that they should haggle over it to such an extent, counting the zeros and commas, while, a stone's throw away at Les Halles, bigger heads of better-fed mammals sell for a pittance. Rakä, indignant, shook the bars of our cage, crying: "Murderers!" but nobody heard him. Mimile, exhausted by his long day, fell asleep every thirty seconds, but the officers continuously shook him awake . . . *

The Queen of Rats flew into a rage and threatened to make use of her supernatural powers to send the humans to be simmered in a pot on the Horn of Africa, which generally frightens Northwesterners, but they were all so busy fighting over Mimile's head that they paid no attention to us, let alone our speeches.** (I've omitted a long passage and will provide you with a summary instead: Mimile is unanimously condemned to death after his lawyer argued that two extenuating circumstances — his mental age and his difficult childhood, which are one and the same — justified the commuting of the guillotine for the more humane electric chair. Mimile, against the counsel of his lawyer, though much to the approval of the rest of the assembly, opted for the guillotine. "We cheered for him, clacking our ears against the bars. Vidvn, however, took advantage of the deliberations to sneak away from the female police officer, run toward us, and, with a flick of her

---

* I have cut two or three monotonous passages heavy on the legalese. —Tr.
** There's something curious about this scene: at no point did the members of the jury become aware of the rats' articulate speech, most likely not believing their ears. Oh, come on! —Tr.

wrist, open our cage: we all rushed out into the hall, where we burst into joyous celebration . . ." In short, the rats manage to escape amidst the general panic their liberation causes in the audience, all while bitterly lamenting the fates of Vidvn and Mimile, for whom they now feel a sincere friendship, with all parties swearing to free each other as soon as circumstances allow, before running across the courtroom where everyone is leaping onto the tables, except for a few cops who give chase, blowing their whistles. Gripping the cables, they slide down to the bottom of the elevator shaft, where the snake, tipped off by who knows what source, awaits them and shows them a secret passageway to the Palais de Justice courtyard.) I quote the letter's conclusion: "The snake, having decided to steal away with us rats, transported us outside as we clung to his back, and slithered us down a tunnel at top speed. When we reached the exit, he said, 'I know someone we could consult: the God of Man. He lives in Sainte-Chapelle—you can see its spire jutting out from inside the Palais de Justice.' The poodle and fox terrier came panting up behind us, having taken advantage of the disorder at the Palais de Justice to bite their guard and break free. Out in the open air now, they started barking and bounding around, biting each other's tail and ears and pissing liberally in the same spots. We called them to order severely, as their frolicking might attract the attention of the mass of humans crowding the Palace gates to call for Mimile's head, and we quickly hid behind a column to watch, on the one hand, Mimile being dragged away by male cops and stuffed in a paddy wagon, and, on the other, Vidvn in the arms of the female cop from before, surrounded by other women dressed in periwinkle, as she was rushed into a white ambulance parked nearby. Then they all drove off through the jeering crowd, which the riot squad calmed down with a few tear gas grenades, the humans coughing and crying the way they do, as everyone knows, when they're prevented from protesting. We waited patiently for the scene to cool off, then we quickly crossed the courtyard with our heads down, following the snake who led the way, slithering between the cobblestones, trailed by the dogs, who trotted in lockstep and, all things considered, were behaving quite well; a judge saw us pass and briefly stopped in his tracks, then shook his wig, thinking he must be dreaming, and we arrived painlessly at the Sainte-Chapelle gate. The snake knocked his head against the door; no answer. The poodle and the fox terrier grew impatient and started peeing on the pedestals. 'Is anybody in there?' cried the snake. Nothing but heavy silence. Suddenly, the door opened and the God of Man appeared, a candle in his hand."

The Ecological God

"GOOD DAY, MY LITTLE ANIMAL FRIENDS," THE GOD OF Man said, and ushered us in with a yawn. "No need for formalities," he added, leading us into Sainte-Chapelle, "take a seat wherever you'd like." The Queen of Rats took her place at the center of the altar and we, the Court, around her, the two princesses sitting upon two censers, and we, the two heirs apparent, beside them, standing on our hind legs, leaning on our tails. The snake wrapped himself around the crucifix, and the fox terrier and poodle, intimidated by the God of Man's presence, sat like earthenware statues on either side of the altar. The God of Man fell asleep, sucking his thumb. With his first snore, he began to levitate, as if he were lying on a transparent air mattress that each snore inflated a bit more, and he rose some twenty feet above us, reaching a space within the Sainte-Chapelle spire, whose thousand-and-one-colored stained glass windows produced a very pleasant kaleidoscopic effect upon this white-bearded man, as hairy as a polar bear. We applauded (mainly to wake him up), and his voice rang out: "I hear you," he said politely but grudgingly, "but I'm warning you," he said, lowering himself slowly back down to the floor, "I'm warning you," he repeated, opening his eyes and mouth wide, "I'm warning you!" he cried out, loud enough to rattle Sainte-Chapelle's stained glass windows, then he stopped, stuck out his thumb, scratched his eye with it, and proceeded to stick it back in his mouth. We understood that this was an incredibly elderly being (two million human years old, according to the snake) who was alive due only to his divine nature; we could expect little from him in terms of help. The poodle and the fox terrier, hypnotized by the human image, approached the god with their heads bowed, wagging their tails in the hope that they might find a master, having already forgotten their old ones, who had died no more than a single day before. He stroked their heads and they shuddered with pleasure, tinkling on the altar. "I've been alone for an eternity," said the God of Man, sniveling. The snake explained to us: "He takes a long time to wake up, passing through successive stages of idiocy. But once he's up, my dears, he's actually quite the conversationalist." The Queen, already eager to get back home to the Square du Vert-Galant, agreed to stay a while longer. Finally, the God of Man rose and dragged his espadrilles over to the confessional booth, took out a gas stove, boiled water for coffee, and offered us some; we politely declined, but the dogs rushed over to the sugar. "You see how I live," he muttered. "They ran me out of all my churches and if I'm still here it's only because they haven't found me yet. It won't be long, though. During visiting hours, I hide under the altar, trembling, so none of those Japanese kids ferret me out." The Queen of Rats declared, in the name of the Court, that we would be very honored if he should agree to come live in our Vert-Galant willow, where he could set up one of his confessionals in the branches, but he politely declined, claiming that he was so used to living in the half light of the stained glass that he could no longer face full daylight. "I even wonder sometimes if I wouldn't go up like a torch in the heat of the Sun," he added, "ever since He got angry with me for turning a profit on some of His personal effects." He drank his coffee slowly; a good amount dripped down the hairs of his beard, which was so long he had to lift it with his hands to keep from stepping on it. "I know you've come here to reproach me," he said, "but I've reproached myself enough already. Instead of driving them out of Eden, I should have stuck them in a cage!" he sobbed, copious tears streaming down his face and into the traces of coffee in his beard. "And what's more, they slandered my friend the Snake," he added, "who never offered them an apple the way they say; they stole it from him after beating him with a makeshift cane — a branch they hacked off my cherry tree with a rock. That was the dessert that followed their first meal in Eden. And I'll tell you the whole menu; they began by force-feeding a goose, stuffing corn cobs down its throat until it choked to death, then they sharpened a stone and cut out its liver; then they killed a rabbit, stringing it up it by its hind legs and bleeding it out entirely through its eye, which they'd pierced with a stone; then they tore off its skin, which Adam used to make himself a cap while Eve braided goose feathers into her hair and smeared her face with blood. To roast the rabbit's corpse, they burned down a pine forest along with the nests of the partridges they devoured along with their eggs, having learned to make fire by rubbing two stones together; they also burned a field of hemp to inhale its smoke, shrieking and running hither and yon, and they tore up my vines to jump on the grapes, urinating on them to draw out a liquid that left them inebriated, and they cut off a goat's teat and devoured it. Their excitement only subsided when they were seized by spasms, with Adam inserting his urinoreproductive member into the ass of a duck while he strangled it, and Eve drinking a donkey's urine before tearing off its sex with a stone and inserting it into her anus; whereupon they fell asleep, splayed out in the nest of an eagle they had decapitated, blanketed by a sheepskin, still warm and dripping with blood. And as soon as they awoke, they stormed my cave and tried to stone me to death because they'd decided to worship a rock they had carved into the shape of a penis." "All you had to do was not create stones!" the Queen of Rats retorted. "Without stones," said the God of Man without skipping a beat, "the earth's ground would melt into diabolical magma, a fiery morass in which all my dear Animals would perish alongside the Humans, and I wouldn't want that." "So, what's your solution?" cried the Queen of Rats in a shrill voice that echoed around Sainte-Chapelle's iridescent and pyramidal vault before fading to a sigh at the heart of the spire. The God of Man stood there stunned for a moment before asking: "My solution to what?" "To yourself!" cried the Queen. "Ah, myself," said the God of Man, "I'm waiting." "Waiting for what?" The God of Man, vexed, walked around the altar, running his hands through his hair, before answering: "I don't know." "Well, I, Sir, do know," said the Queen of Rats haughtily, settled on her hind legs in the middle of the altar, swaying her hips: "You're waiting for Death, just like the rest of us!" I was worried he would get angry, but he did nothing of the sort; instead, he changed his tone, his voice suddenly beyond age and gender. "I'm waiting for death," he said, "but I know it's not coming tomorrow. As long as they remember me, even if only to hate me ... And such is my punishment, the sin of Creation was within me, even before they existed." And he began to weep again in silence. "But why did you create THEM?" said the Queen of Rats. "I needed a couple of gardeners for my Eden," he said, "and anyway, that's how just about every other species was created (and I dare say humans aren't the only failures, all creation is a risk), since Eden belongs to a succession of different gods, of which I'm the last, since the God of Gods was so disappointed by me that he swore off having any more children." "I understand that," said the Queen, "but of all the atrocities that have been committed, you'll agree the most glaring is the construction of cities! They always build them in our territories — and only in our territories — and very few of our kingdoms escape them! And all that because of your damned stones, which they've even learned to produce themselves now!" The God of Man lowered his eyes, humiliated, and set about braiding the hairs of his beard with his old, shaky fingers. "We can't expect a thing from him," exclaimed the Queen. "We'll never be able to expect a thing from him," said the Snake, speaking for the first time, "that's not what he's good for, but now we know." "Know what?" asked the Queen. "That we'll never be able to expect a thing from him," the Snake replied, quite rightly. Seeing the God of Man so sad, the fox terrier and the poodle went to rub up against his knees to comfort him, licking at the traces of sweet coffee in his beard. We, the Rat Court and the snake, left Sainte-Chapelle with our heads held high, but not without the Queen of Rats snapping at the God of Man, "You can keep the dogs, God!" before slamming the door, and we found ourselves back out in the fresh air. When Rakä threw some stones to break Sainte-Chapelle's stained glass windows, I followed his lead; we all burst out laughing, letting go of all our fear.

The Rat Devil

IT WAS A BEAUTIFUL DAY OUTSIDE. WE LAY IN THE SUN for a while. "Let's go for groceries down at the flower market," said the Queen of Rats, "before we head back to the Square du Vert-Galant. I'd like to put some geraniums out on my willow." "But first let's swing by the quay for some canaries, I'm starving," said the snake. Just then an explosion blasted Sainte-Chapelle into tiny pieces, which fell down all around us; thankfully, we were standing behind a column that protected us. When the smoke cleared, we pointed our muzzles and saw, where Sainte-Chapelle had just stood, a crater drooling fiery lava and a rather compact column of black smoke rising high into the sky, where the God of Man was standing on one leg, his other crossed, like a stork; our friends the poodle and fox terrier, decked out in white wings, buzzed like flies around him, then quickly disappeared into the azure. The earth began to spew red lava, then cracked open, making way for the Rat Devil's red ears to rise to the surface; he promptly climbed out and plugged the crater with his immense derrière before bursting into such uproarious laughter that every window pane in Paris shattered. Breathing fire from his nostrils, he roared: "You, poor Rats, have been chosen by me, the Rat Devil, to found a City of Rats where all good-willed men shall find their place beside you!" Then he exploded like a lava-filled bladder hurling enormous fireballs onto the nearby riverbanks, setting ablaze the Académie Française and the Louvre. The Île de la Cité broke away from the river bottom; the bridges connecting it to the banks of Paris and the Île Saint-Louis collapsed, toppling heavily into the river; Notre-Dame swayed on its foundations and the island began to drift away, pushed by the current toward the Pont des Arts, which fell, crushing the Île's first row of houses; a swarm of tourists, locals, lawyers, cops, and clergymen rushed out of the Palais de Justice, the Prefecture, and Notre-Dame, stranding the prisoners in their underground cells. They threw themselves into the water and swam for the banks, some on ad hoc rafts made of doors; the barges and human river firefighters fished a few of them out, but many drowned, having thrown themselves into the water without knowing how to swim. On the other hand, the Parisian city rats dove into the water and swam toward us, cutting through the humans and biting them as they passed. The island was soon devoid of humans but full of rats who belted out our old revolutionary songs. Two helicopters approaching the island exploded in midair, as did the dozen police boats that tried to pull up on our shores, which demonstrated to all present that we were under the protection of a being of either divine or diabolical nature, or some alliance of the two; this was confirmed by the precision with which the Île de la Cité took the river's curves at cruising speed. We all ran toward Notre-Dame, the Queen of Rats at the head, the snake bringing up the rear, and climbed to its highest balcony, from which the Queen gave a brief speech to the crowd, introducing Rakä and me as her heirs apparent, and the snake, coiled around a gargoyle, as her Prime Minister, requesting with great sincerity that those down on the Parvis go free the humans imprisoned in the basements of the Palais de Justice, the Prefecture of Police, the Hôpital Sainte-Anne, and the Hôtel-Dieu. The crowd of rats, swarming far below us, broke into discussions. "These humans are like us," cried Rakä, "the proof: they've been imprisoned by humans!" "It's a very serious risk," a voice cried, but the majority decided to obey us after a vote. "In any event, we outnumber them and have the cops' weapons (three rats can fire a rifle just as ably as three men can fire a cannon), plus, given that the prisoners and the sick are unarmed, we have the advantage." It was moving to see these two or three thousand humans emerge from their cells into the light of day. The Queen of Rats, from atop Notre-Dame, greeted them, wished them well, and briefly outlined the situation at hand, whereupon they all gave us a standing ovation, crying and laughing, kissing each other and rats alike; Rakä and I rang the cathedral bells, hanging from the ropes. That's when Mimile came bounding up the tower stairs four by four with Vidvn (whom he'd just picked up from the Hôtel-Dieu) in his arms, both overflowing with joy, and he cried, "My memory came back after the Event!" And so it was for all the human beings, who now remembered their every act and deed since birth; of their close associates, they remembered less, although some did recall bits and pieces of the lives of ancestors who had been dead for a thousand human centuries, and others even started physically reproducing their grandmothers' gestures. They were telling each other the stories of their lives loud and fast, and the clamor rose up to us. The rats did the same amongst themselves and with the humans; soon, everyone came to think they could understand each other, as everyone's life was similar, differing only in their decorative elements, which were quite distinct, but this was the result, they claimed, of a deformation of vision that had befallen us before the Event. As for me, I was hesitant to support this theory, as my memory hadn't changed and differed from theirs in that I remembered the lives of others better than my own, and I was even able to describe them.*

As the Île de la Cité sped along, we could already feel the sea breeze and everyone was throwing together warmer outfits as night swiftly approached; the prisoners covered themselves in the old rags of judges, priests, and doctors, the rats whipped up nice, warm vests by cutting two holes in lawyers' wigs, and the snake crafted a sheath by stitching up the edges of two priestly stoles. We, the Queen and the Rat Court, decided to spend the night in the Archbishop's chambers in Notre-Dame, where a closed-circuit TV network connected us to every part of the island, because we feared a UN attack in the night. We didn't sleep a wink, given the general commotion that had taken hold of Notre-Dame and the Parvis. After the prisoners had broken into the archbishop's wine cellar, they threw a champagne-soaked party in the nave of the cathedral. Nine madwomen from the Sainte-Anne mental asylum played the organ together and the others drank and fornicated all over, humans and rats together; Vidvn and other children of her age, in the arms of Mimile and a number of his hobo companions, danced around their bonfires on the Parvis until, deep in the night, they fell asleep wherever they so happened to pass out, and all fell still. The only sound was the wind blowing us out to sea. Mimile came to join us in the

---

* I find this passage to be in the poor taste of a writer unafraid to boast; it's certainly not from the books I showed him that he fell under this influence. —Tr.

Archbishop's bed and fell asleep beside us after vomiting wine on the purple carpet; he was holding Vidvn, who sucked her thumb as she slept. We grunted in disapproval of his behavior, but he was already snoring. The snake, coiled around the chandelier, bid us good night, and turned off the lights by unscrewing the bulbs with his tail. I fell into a fitful sleep, and I dreamed of you, Master, sitting atop a coconut tree.

The Emir of Parrots

I ROSE EARLY IN THE MORNING TO FINISH MY PREVIOUS letter with one of the archbishop's metal-tipped quills, which I dipped in a blue liquid; to write, I sat on a tower of Notre-Dame where the sun beat down so hard it made you forget the ocean breeze; the shore was far out of sight now, and the horizon described a perfect circle around us. We had advanced a great distance in the night; for the first time in my life, my body delighted in what they call a tropical climate. The waves of the sea, bluer than the sky, caressed the banks of the Île de la Cité, the stony colors of which adorned themselves in reflections in a range of colors from red to transparent, passing by way of green; our willow tree at the island's prow shook its hair voluptuously in the wind and a flock of seagulls escorted us along, squawking their bienvenue to the waters. An albatross alighted beside me, blowing my papers to the ground. "You must be the Rat Court," he said breathlessly, "I have a message for you, on behalf of the Emir of Parrots." I was about to unfold the parchment he had handed me when Rakä came running over: "Gouri," he said, "I think the earth is flooded!" "Haven't you heard?" asked the albatross, surprised, "it's the flood!" "But it didn't rain a drop last night," replied Rakä. "And rightly so! All the elements turned to liquid after midnight, and not only the clouds, but the eternal ice, too. The sea has covered the earth!" "But why?" I asked. "The axis the world spins on has gone mad, it's spinning every which way like a baton those curious American ex-women known as cheerleaders use to grab the attention of the crowds. Right now the sun is beating down everywhere and the world is one great ball of ocean; the only bit of land still afloat is your Île de la Cité, who knows why! The sea is teeming with ships in distress: oil tankers, aircraft carriers, fishing boats, leisure craft, and all other kinds, which, believe me, will survive only a short time without recourse to land. In his letter, the Emir of Parrots warns you of the imminent danger of invasion by boats flying human flags, and cordially requests you to place yourselves under his protection. I personally urge you to listen! Look, on the horizon, the Americans are coming!" he pointed with his enormous wings. It was true, and, much closer yet, we noticed the periscopes of Russian spy submarines. "To arms!" cried Rakä from the top of Notre-Dame down to the humans and rats, still sleeping in puddles of their own vomit from last night's feast, scattered all around the Île de la Cité. The Queen of Rats arrived at the top of Notre-Dame with her hair full of curlers, crying hysterically: "What's happening, what's happening?" We quickly explained the situation to her after introducing the albatross as the Emir of Parrots' ambassador; the two princesses arrived in turn at the tower, squealing with fright; we hid them prudently inside a gargoyle. Whether it was the unexpected situation or the sea air, the humans and rats were quickly awake and alert: under Rakä's leadership, the humans destroyed the upper floors of the Palais de Justice with pickaxes in order to secure the island's perimeter with barricades, while the rats assisted them, carrying stones on their backs like mules. "Where's my Prime Minister?" cried the Queen of Rats. "Here," the snake answered calmly, curled up beside her. "What should we do?" asked the Queen. "Nothing," answered the snake; "they'll never dare attack us because they don't understand how we can possibly move without a motor, they think we have energy sources unknown to them, and thus weapons capable of destroying theirs. They certainly believe we're the ones behind the flood!" We all laughed, albeit nervously. The rats and the humans took up positions behind the barricades, the humans with rifles and the rats with knives between their teeth, ready to board the enemy ships. The American fleet was soon close enough for us to discern its men, all dressed in white and standing erect in formation on the decks; as for the Russian submarines, they remained underwater, occasionally cruising around or underneath the island before breaching the surface with their periscopes, in the lenses of which we could see their stunned blue eyes. "Here comes the Emir of Parrots to save the day!" announced the albatross, pointing to the sky with his beak and kneeling with great difficulty as he joined his wings together; far up in the sky we glimpsed a small point of light like the head of a pin with fly wings, which, as it approached, zigzagging in front of the sun (which to our eyes, by who knows what optical aberration, remained perpetually at its zenith), resolved into focus as a multicolored parrot who came crashing into us, knocking over the Queen of Rats, who had no time to get out of the way, before somersaulting away and bashing his head on a column in a cloud of feathers and jewels. Of all the parrots I have seen, this was the most sumptuously adorned. His iridescent golden head was topped by a scarlet turban with a large sapphire over his forehead, his beak was a marbled pink, his motley yellow and green wings were attached to a midnight-blue body which ended in three white feathers on his tail, all set on legs that were rather hideous (as is true of all birds). Aside from his turban, he wore a silk vest embroidered with a thousand precious stones and a pearl necklace tied insouciantly around his waist as a belt. The albatross threw himself to the ground in prostration before repeating three times: "Behold the Wingèd Emir!" I was immediately suspicious of this strange character: he claimed to have arrived with neither vehicle nor escort because his parakeets had been taken prisoner by an owl, his flying carpet stolen, apparently, by a condor, and he offered the Queen a little ruby jewel bearing, assuring her that it was the most beautiful of all his treasures. Even the tone of his voice struck us as imported, and the scar around his ankle outed him as an ex-convict. The albatross unfolded a rough map of the Île de la Cité and the parrot tapped his claw on the Conciergerie and the Hôtel-Dieu, which he was ready to purchase in exchange for his protection and a tiny purse in which he jingled two sous. His protection? It was of the Islamic sort, and he couldn't reveal the secret of what it consisted in; the snake stood firm on this point: the island belonged to land animals and we saw no reason to cede so much as a single square inch of it to fowl, although we would allow them to perch on the buildings and trees for a tithe to be determined according to each bird's means, for example, the parakeets of his escort as appetizers. The queen wanted a diamond for her crown, and Iris and Carina demanded the parrot's turban to make a nest for our litters; the negotiations escalated; Rakä took me aside, saying: "This is complete nonsense, Gouri. Let's go see what's happening down on the square." We left the Court middiscussion with the parrot and albatross on a tower of Notre-Dame. As we scampered down the stairs, Rakä voiced his concerns: Sooner or later the human armies would attack us, although, he said without much conviction, maybe we could count on a mutiny of all the rats in the ships flying human banners, and their alliance; nothing more likely. And we would surely emerge from the confrontation as the sole losers; if they spared the humans' lives (which was quite possible, even if they sent them back to Sainte-Anne and the prison cells), they would gladly exterminate us rats. We couldn't count on the Emir of Parrots, a true snake-oil salesman if I'd ever seen one and clearly no Emir, just a parrot from the slums, as his way of talking demonstrated, though we did, on the other hand, consider the possibility of making our escape on the albatross, who could carry the entire Rat Court on his wings, plus the snake wrapped around his neck; but beside the fact that the albatross was clearly under the parrot's orders, we were loath to abandon the others, and we decided to help them leave in case of emergency—if Rakä and I had to surrender all our possessions to the parrot and remain on the island, so be it; this gambit so seduced us that we were soon unable to imagine any alternative, even though it meant almost certain death. We told each other that we probably would never meet our children, but then again we hadn't met our own fathers, and that hadn't stopped us from living lives we were proud of, given the diversity of our adventures. We thought that the waters would recede—this was not the earth's first flood—and Iris and Carina would return to the shore on the albatross's wings to give birth to new rats who, this time around, just maybe, would be able to live in peace with humans and cats, all having learned a lesson from the flood, although deep down we had our reservations, and experience soon proved us right.

The Rat Orator

DOWN ON THE PARVIS NOTRE-DAME, WE FOUND THE humans and rats in dispute, all their hackles raised. The rats were accusing the humans of decapitating a rat with their teeth (which was true, though one of the madwomen from Sainte-Anne was behind it), and threatened them with razors, which they brandished with their tails; the humans, all haggard and riled up, called the rats pigs for eating the corpse of a young man who had died of an overdose, leaving nothing but his tibia and hair. When they saw us coming, they all fell silent, the rats huddling together in the middle of the square and the humans parading around us with rifles over their backs, except for Mimile and Vidvn, who stood with the rats, having sworn to defend them against the humans, plus a few turncoat rodents who showboated on the humans' rifles and shoulders. Rakä asked them all to be silent, and they quieted down. "Brothers," he cried at the top of his lungs against the sea wind, "this is no time to fight amongst ourselves!" A human stepped forward and spat on the ground at our feet, and we all jumped back. He took out a switchblade and threatened us: "If one more rat dares touch us again, I'll throw each and every one of you to the sharks!" Then he spat again, this time on me. They had locked up some of the madwomen from Sainte-Anne down in their prison cells for fornicating with rats, but chose to keep on the turncoat rats who served them so courteously now, cleaning their shoes and rifles and performing other humiliating tasks (which I'll omit) like so many dogs, hoping in this way to survive the invasion of the human armies and receive the compensation of lodging in the holds of their ships, per tradition. I overcame my fear and said, in a nevertheless tremulous voice: "Sire" (the man was clearly Anglo-Saxon, with tomato-colored skin and ginger hair), "Sire"—I repeated until he heard me, silencing the laughter of the human crowd with the wave of his hand—"if war must be waged among humans, we rats can offer no remedy. And though we, upon this drifting city, may be of different species, our mutual interest is survival. Peace is essential to all of us." The rats broke into applause, joined by a few dissident humans. This filled me with courage, and I went on with my speech: "There is surely an end to all life, our common ground, but the very nature of the time we have makes us wary of it, not knowing from which end it might be grasped. I propose to you that we live united until our deaths, placing our trust in eternity, which is to time what the cat is to the mouse, however difficult death may be." A man came to shake my paw, congratulating me on my eloquence, and an old hippie woman began singing Afro-Indian melodies to the accompaniment of an acoustic guitar. "Humans under all banners," I resumed, "seek our destruction and your imprisonment; we must cultivate our superiority by combining our wits: every man who has spent part of his life in a prison cell against his will shall be an honorary rat; every rat who can speak, an honorary human." I received even more applause at the end of this rejoinder, the tone of which recalled to some of the humans their old, yet still vivid, dreams of fraternity. They compromised and agreed to maintain our alliance until the armies invaded; at which point, they said, "God will decide." We protested, their gods being if not dead then wholly absent, while our Devil, quite to the contrary, was still blowing us toward safe harbor. They laughed in our faces: suddenly, we saw the Rat Devil rise up over Notre-Dame, one hind leg on each tower and his forelegs on his hips, booming with laughter and whipping the sea with his tail. This terrified everyone but us; the humans scrambled away to hide in their dungeons. "Good riddance," cried Rakä, "to bad rubbish!" and we rats prostrated before the Rat Devil who assumed the position of Buddha, resting his knees on the towers of Notre-Dame. His voice was muffled: "As long as I am the master of this ship's winds," he bellowed, blowing fire from his ears and pointing straight at me, "I will accept no despicable fools under my command!" I blushed, confused, unsure how I had betrayed him. "Gouri, your days are numbered! For nearly an entire day of rat life now, I have granted you my City, and what have you done with it? I see the humans rushing into the labyrinths, frightened by my very sight, and you, my rats, I see you bickering!" I kept silent and prostrated until my ears touched the floor, though I still couldn't see what I was guilty of. "You're wasting your time, you lout," the Rat Devil cried, before vanishing like a cloud of smoke. The rats gathered around me, asking me what this apparition had meant, and I confessed to them that I didn't understand it myself, when suddenly it hit me: the Rat Devil was simply asking me to annihilate the human armies! In all likelihood, that was the meaning of his reproach; we all agreed on this point, but how could we do it? With the cooperation of the ex-prisoner humans we could have laid a trap to lure them to the island and take a number of their leaders hostage, but we obviously couldn't count on our humans, beaten down by prison life and quite possibly born cowards. We held a vote on whether or not to lock them back up in their cells and almost unanimously decided that they should remain free, given that they were now as afraid of the Rat Devil as we had been of their God back in the days of their kingdom. And yet, these poor wretches were waiting for us to lock them back up, each having returned to his cell of his own accord; after we had sent Mimile to them as our ambassador, with Vidvn in his arms, they all came back up to the square repenting their wickedness and confessing to all imaginable crimes, rending their chests and declaring their submission to the Rat Devil. "If he's so powerful, this damn devil," I was wondering, "why doesn't he just annihilate the armies himself?" when I heard the voice of the Rat Devil inside my head, though the others couldn't hear it: "Because you're the chosen one, you filthy little cretin!" he shouted, deafening me. This method of his shocked me and I hastened to tell my audience about it, swearing to them that under no circumstances would I obey his word without their general consent. The Queen of Rats and the Court came down the stairs of Notre-Dame with little baskets to go shopping at the flower market as if it were just a day like any other, a move which clearly demonstrated her sagacity; this little stroke of humor relaxed us and made the whole crowd smile. But out on the Parvis, she has a change of heart and starts ordering everyone around, commanding a big picnic in the sunshine at noon and inviting the humans to strip naked, the better to enjoy the sunlight, but cautiously, as the whiter ones among them tend to burn easily. The snake also added orders to the order of the order, if I dare say: he organized a thorough cleaning of the Île de la Cité, which was filthy from yesterday's orgy, judiciously dividing up the tasks between the humans and rats; the humans swept the ground and the rats cleaned Notre-Dame, squeezing into the nooks and crannies of the stone, and scrubbing it with their fur; in less than an hour, our cathedral was as clean as a freshly minted sou. The picnic was thrown together quickly on purple tablecloths, using the silver dishware of the Archbishop of Paris, which we laid out upon the square; as for food, we were quickly reassured on this point: the Rat Devil showered us with a vast array of foodstuffs, ranging from corn on the cob to a steaming, bloody leg of lamb for the humans, and for us rats a specimen of every cheese and bread produced in the world; for the Emir of Parrots, chickpeas, which he refused as he joined our table; for the albatross a sardine so salty it made him cough. As for the snake, he was granted a nice, green iguana. After ringing the bells of Notre-Dame, we, the court and notables, moved to the center tablecloth, where the iguana was already struggling for his life under a cheese cloche beside our cloches with cheeses inside, Vidvn had a nice bottle of whipped cow's milk with honey, and Mimile a big hamburger with lots of ketchup, all washed down with a light, resinated wine. Before sitting at the table, we thanked the Rat Devil and, out of good manners, the God of Man; the madwomen from Sainte-Anne invoked their goddess Diana, the parrot Allah. The parrot, to my left, ate my entire plate while I was speaking softly with Rakä, to my right: although we had momentarily found ourselves at ease, the American aircraft carriers and Russian submarines were getting closer and closer to our shores, their curiosity overcoming their fear, especially since the Rat Devil had appeared with his rain of food, possibly mistaking us for a projection of one of those stupid cartoons that so grotesquely distort their way of thinking. We decided to make a speech at the end of the meal to assure our continued alliance with a share of the humans, whose goodwill we recognized, now that they had room and board and freedom to roam in the sun. Rakä, during the meal, took notes for my speech; our two wives Iris and Carina chatted with their mother, the Queen of Rats, likening our adventure to a Mediterranean cruise they'd taken last summer, which they recounted in detail to the albatross. The snake lifted the cheese cloche and looked into the eyes of the iguana frozen in fear. The snake stuck out his forked tongue, licking the scaly snout of the iguana, who, in turn, stuck out his own and licked the snake's eyes; the snake, moved by a humanitarian sentiment, spared the iguana's life, and they shared a plate of goat cheese. We were all praising his gesture when the iguana leapt at the Emir of Parrots, mistaking him for part of the feast; before we could pull the parrot free from the iguana's mouth, the parrot had lost all his tail feathers and his turban, which the iguana had devoured. We returned the iguana to his cheese cloche and sat back down, trying to calm the Emir, whose heart was beating wildly; to recover, he downed a whole glass of gin in one gulp. Mimile drank a little too much and led a group of gypsies to ransack the archives of the Palais de Justice, setting fire to a mountain of files in the courtyard before doing the same to the archive of the Préfecture de Police and the Archbishop's library, where the majority of books were obscene in nature. I was the only one to disapprove of their action, which I was unable to prevent. Wherever you looked, a human memory was going up in smoke; with this act, they scorned their own God. I found something repugnant in their submission to the Rat Devil, his beneficence aside. I suspected the Devil would intervene and put a stop to their book burning, but he did nothing of the sort; quite to the contrary, he howled with laughter inside my head. Taking offense, I finished my café calva and smoked a hashish cigarette that a hairy Dutchman sitting alone upon a step of Notre-Dame offered me while this band of goons lit fires all around us; the rats, in their drunkenness, joined the humans. I summoned the Court, the Emir, and our Prime Minister to the archbishop's library, the empty shelves of which were a sorry sight, and we sat down on the desk; the albatross splayed himself out in an armchair and fell asleep, letting the parrot speak for him. Ultimately, it wasn't a question of voting, but of getting everyone to pledge their complete solidarity. The snake moved to state his case first. Given his sympathy for the iguana, he had hardly eaten at all, but now he wanted to reconsider his decision, he said, lifting with his tail the cheese cloche where the iguana lay sleeping, and before we could say a word he had gobbled him right up. The iguana contorted inside the snake, who contorted in turn until the both of them shook with spasms; the iguana expired and the snake, rather plump now, climbed with difficulty to the highest shelf of the library where he fell asleep, snoring loudly. Our wives Iris and Carina were terrified by this spectacle, and we had to calm them with some belladonna suppositories we scrounged up in the archbishop's medicine cabinet, and we laid them to bed. Mimile came in with a bottle of Préfontaines under one arm and Vidvn naked in the other, his clothes almost burnt, belting out: "Ah! Ça ira! Ça ira! Ça ira! Les aristocrates à la lanterne!" Vidvn, who was by all appearances drunk, was laughing and shouting "Peepee! poopoo!" and relieving herself on Mimile, who lapped up her excrement and urine. They were called harshly to order by the Queen of Rats, who sent them to wash up in the swimming pool in the archbishop's bathroom. They went off with their heads hanging low, but as soon as they were in the tub, they started playing with the shower head, laughing and blowing water out of their noses; we opted to close the door and return to our discussions, which were becoming increasingly urgent, since the human armies had launched a smoke bomb during this whole commotion, and everyone on the island was hacking and coughing. We returned to the office; the Emir of Parrots helped himself to one of the archbishop's Cuban cigars, which he dipped in a cup of cognac before lighting it with a large gold lighter and, blowing the smoke in our faces as he held the cigar in his disgusting claw, said to the Queen of Rats, Rakä, and myself: "Your plan is my plan." I answered: "Your plan is your own and not ours, Emir; try talking straight, for once in your life. You understand our situation as well as we do: you know that outside our Île de la Cité your survival, and that of your companions, is simply not possible, and the human armies know this, too. Any given square inch of this land is more valuable, Emir, than all your rags combined. At this point, our only hope is to establish peace among everyone on the island (especially among the notables, such as yourself) regardless of who's who, since we all share a plan." "Well put," murmured the distracted Queen, who in the meantime had found a ball of purple wool and was playing with it. "But what is this plan of yours?" the parrot snapped mockingly. "Well put," repeated the ever more distracted queen. "My plan with Rakä is to combine our wits, so that we animals don't fall into their traps, as has happened so many times over the course of our history." The Emir of Parrots shook his head, laughing to himself. "My dear rat," he said, "it's not a matter of traps, but of weapons, which are much faster. I'm not optimistic about your fate, but mine is already an old tale: everyone knows that a parrot capable of pronouncing dirty words in multiple languages will automatically become the human army's mascot" (and he recited a few, to demonstrate); "for me, it's not a matter of life and death. Sure, I'll be your ally," he added, "but only because I've always dreamed of their extinction. Still, I have my limits: neither I nor the albatross will die by your side, rats, or by anyone else's." "Well put," murmured the albatross between snores, the Queen having woken him up by hitting him with her ball of wool. Suddenly, three cannon shots rattled the windowpanes and we ran to the archbishop's windows; the two fat, platinum-haired chiefs of the American and Russian armies were standing in the middle of the Parvis Notre-Dame with the two fleets in formation on either side of the island. Our humans were scattering in all directions to hide. We decided to open the cathedral doors and let them in.

The Atheist Rat

SINCE THE ONLY HUMANS WITH US WERE VIDVN AND Mimile, we told Mimile to put on the archbishop's robes and sit on the cathedral's organ. Vidvn, dressed like an altar girl, which suited her ebony skin nicely, fell asleep almost immediately on Mimile's lap. We rats fashioned ourselves tights out of the Archbishop's lilac stockings, and the Emir of Parrots, in all his jewels, took his place on the head of the albatross, who was spreading his wings at the center of the nave. The Queen of Rats, in her anxiety, couldn't stop playing with her ball of wool, rolling it into every corner of Notre-Dame while our two absent-minded wives complained of migraines, the absent-minded snake by their side (we hadn't been able to wake him). We had two madwomen from Sainte-Anne open the doors; they had meanwhile entered into our service, dressed as abbesses. The two Russian and American commanders-in-chief, both blond and identical in appearance, stepped forward, arm in arm. Two dark-haired interpreters of the female sex walked behind them, their teeth bared in a rictus imitating the smiling expression that is, for us rats, only natural. Their courtesy was so forced that we immediately realized that these men were more afraid of some unknown power than they were of us. They whacked their temples with their right index fingers as they contracted every muscle in their bodies, and their interpreters introduced them to us as

Admirals Smutchenko and Smith. At first, we heard "animals" instead of "admirals" and requested that the interpreters repeat themselves—they spoke truly execrable French. We ordered our good Sainte-Anne madwomen to serve them tea or coffee per their taste, and invited them to sit to our left and right on benches in the nave. The parrot asked to read their palms and took this opportunity to steal their wedding rings, while the interpreters, still smiling, explained that they were waiting for their chiefs to get divorced so they could marry them, and other such nonsense; we made it clear that we wanted them to leave, that this was indispensable if we were to found the City of Rats. They conveyed our demands to their chiefs, serving their chiefs as interpreters, until they informed us that, under the circumstances, they would be acting as our escort. But to protect us from what and to go where? They agreed in unison in their respective languages that the waters would end up receding and that land, air, and sea would once again be divided, and that they would keep their share (the air, land, and sea, as usual). The Emir of Parrots burst out laughing, as did we rats. If we couldn't yet call the sea creatures our allies, they were in even worse standing, and for good reason, since their warships terrorized all sorts of fish, who currently kept their distance but were liable to come to our aid at a moment's notice, the Emir of Parrots assured us. Not least the sawfish, the albatross's longtime friends, who could pierce holes in their ships, if need be. The American chief, exasperated, asked to speak directly to Mimile, taking him for our leader. Mimile was hanging from the organ pipes and lifted his cassock, flashing his posterior to all, and Vidvn ran over to pee on the American interpreter's shoe. They began talking nervously amongst themselves in Russian and

English. Our two fine madwomen asked the interpreters for their caps as a gift, which they promptly handed over. The American chief stood up and coughed. He asked if he might visit our nuclear facilities; we explained that our island had no engine, but that we relied on the protection of the Rat Devil, who suddenly appeared, shattering one of Notre-Dame's rose windows with his tail and, at great length, pissing boiling-hot urine on the Russian and American chiefs before he began to speak.

(Translator's note: I thought it best to cut the following passage, which is marked by a useless cruelty, and to provide you with a summary instead: The Russian and American armies are swiftly annihilated by the Rat Devil, who thereby assures his patronage of Gouri before disappearing in the customary fiery fart. The human ex-convicts and the rats, who have been joined by a few sailors, watch the last boats floating near the island's barricades burn into the sea while the sun goes down; after killing their two interpreters with pistols, the two admirals commit suicide with cyanide pills, each professing the hope that they might find each other again in the afterlife — knowing the God of Man's thoughts on the subject, Gouri said, nothing was less likely. I leave the credibility of this passage to the reader's judgment. I quote the final part of this letter:)

It's night, Master, and I'm writing by moonlight. All are sleeping but the dead, whom I mourn, yet whose deaths were inevitable from the Rat Devil's perspective. I have decided to break with him, considering that, in his place, I would have found a more suitable, if not quite so spectacular, solution. Both rats and men have lost their interest for me, as have their gods, devils, and discourses. My friend Rakä is losing his personality before my eyes, the Queen of Rats is becoming downright idiotic, and our two wives, Iris and Carina, are falling sick with a resentment that will be impossible to uproot. The Emir of Parrots has dozed off in the albatross's wings after sodomizing him, and snores so loudly now that the occupants of the neighboring houses have woken up and decided to go sleep elsewhere. I miss our conversations, Master, however much I've come to doubt their usefulness, although the word *usefulness* means nothing to me anymore. A tear streams down my muzzle, slides over my whiskers, and falls upon this page. This adventure is my life, it's true, and I wouldn't trade it for any other, but it comes at the cost of having lost the innocent pleasure I once took in watching the leaves glide across the water while eating a paper cone of fries under a bridge on the Seine, holding it with the tip of my tail, an innocence, alas, that I shall never find again, so tense has my brain become since I watched the human armies burn alive under the fiery jets of lava the Rat Devil spewed upon them from his anus, and I instinctively fell to my knees and prayed, believing that their god would perhaps spare their lives. The Rat Devil gave us no time to negotiate with these people, having no faith in my oratory skills. I was writing these lines when I saw the Rat Devil appear, the size of a ladybug on the tip of my snout. "Gouri," he said in a gentle voice, "I've done the hard work for you, for I am your father whom you never knew; I raped your poor white virgin mouse of a mother in the gutter of the Rue de l'Ancienne-Comédie one maniacal night; if you owe your life to me, then I owe you a helping hand . . . This is the second-to-last time you will see me," he said, "the waters will recede tomorrow; good luck!" And off he went, flying away past the full moon like a ladybug with the tiny ears and tail of a rat. It was chilly and I was the only one awake on the island. I took the opportunity to roll up this piece of parchment I stole from the archbishop and stick a stamp on it, which I grabbed from my wallet out of habit, thinking that you were almost certainly dead and that I was most likely writing these letters for nobody, however much I held onto the hope that you had survived the flood on that inflatable boat you used to bring along on your August holidays in Sète, the one you kept under your bed and upon which, perhaps, someday, I hope to see you land on our shores—and yet, I reasoned with myself, with your three broken ribs . . . Unable to sleep, I wandered the island wrapped in a pair of the archbishop's warm, woolly, lilac underwear, redolent of lavender. Our rats and humans were asleep in their apartments; I wandered the crenelations of the now useless barricades, contemplating the still-smoldering wrecks of the Russian and American militaries. A white whale followed us in the wake of the Île de la Cité, piloted by a penguin in a blue woolen navy cap he'd scavenged from the disaster. The whale, who spoke while blowing torrents of water through his teeth and a bidet-like jet from his back, literally inundated me before I could understand a word. The penguin almost drowned in a whirlpool and came to shake out his short wings beside me. "Where's the albatross?" the whale asked me. At first I thought he had said, "Shalom!" and I continued, crying out, "Welcome!" When I realized he was the albatross's friend, I shouted: "He's sleeping." "He can't go on like this," spat the whale, "he abandoned his wife and children—my godchildren—at the North Pole, to chase after a tropical parrot! Bring him here right now, that lecher!" I explained as calmly as I could that the albatross was our guest and that it would be uncivil to wake him during the night, whereupon I bid the whale good evening and went back up the stairs of the quay. The whale called me a homo and a slut, soaking me with water, but I shrugged it off. I tiptoed back into the archbishop's quarters; everyone was asleep, Vidvn and Mimile with the Rat Court in the archbishop's bed and the snake drowsing on the library's top shelf; I knew from the creaking of the archbishop's rocking chair in the dark that the Emir of Parrots was sodomizing the albatross. Slipping into the bathroom, I undressed and dried my fur. When I looked up at my reflection in the mirror, I recoiled. I'd lost most of my fur, leaving only the fur on my scalp, my ears were plastered to my temples, my once-aquiline snout had shrunk into an upturned nose like a man's, along with the rest of my face, my tiny mouth was framed by the hemorrhoids you humans call lips, which made me vomit with disgust, and my body began to grow into the image of a man. I collapsed, sobbing, in the sink, when I saw the Rat Devil, now the size of a cockroach, pop out of the drain, circling in the swirl of my vomit and tears, and he said to me, with a laugh, "This is the last time you'll see me, Gouri," before he let himself wash down the drain in the increasingly iridescent, spiraling current. I looked in the mirror and saw myself as I really was: a handsome, plump young rat, with a healthy coat of fur. I turned out the bathroom light and went to nestle with my companions in the archbishop's bed, right up against Rakä. The Queen of Rats slid between my legs and sucked my penis to no effect; I fell into a heavy sleep, I dreamed of nothing.

Disneyland

TRANSLATOR'S NOTE: I RECEIVED THE PREVIOUS LETters in the spring of '78; I've already informed you of the circumstances. The following letters arrived a year later, I append them to the second edition of this collection. In the interim, I had left my flat on 16 Rue de Buci to live in the countryside with a sweet woman who, I hope, will be my companion until the end of my days. I could never quite tell what parts of this story are real or imaginary, maybe due to a lack of curiosity. Nevertheless, when I received these letters I felt a pang of regret that I never got to know Gouri better (I hope not to bore you by referring to strictly personal matters that have nothing to do with the story), whom I met on the sidewalk of the Rue Dauphine as I was walking out of a bar one winter night in the middle of a nervous breakdown. I saw, as I've said, a litter of newborn rats in a garbage can, and I picked one up and put him in my pocket before walking home. I can't explain why I did it, I might have just been lonely. I had handed the last of my money over zinc counters and I didn't have enough for lunch the next day, a friend of mine having promised to pay me back some money he owed me, but not until later on. I got ready to read, leaving the little rat by the gas heater, when he hopped up and stood in front of me, spreading out his ears; I read to him aloud from who knows what, having a hilarious time until I passed out, dead drunk. The next day, Gouri (I was the one who gave him that name, it seemed so pretty for a rat) woke me up by bringing me my bottle of gin in bed, dragging it by the neck, before hauling over a book he had chosen from my library because of its illustrations; it was an H. G. Wells sci-fi novel that I love; you can imagine what followed. He stayed at my place for a while, eating my leftovers, and I read my entire little library aloud to him. In the evenings, I took him out with me to the bars on Saint-Germain-des-Prés with a pink ribbon around his neck, which made the men laugh and frightened the women; although everyone ended up getting a kick out of it when I asked for a bébé au lait with a straw for him, and a gin and tonic for myself. I met my now-wife one early May morning when, completely sauced, I recited to Gouri the most beautiful poem I know, in my execrable Spanish accent:

> *Recuerde el alma dormida,*
> *Avive el seso y despierte*
> *Contemplando*
> *Cómo se pasa la vida,*
> *Cómo se viene la muerte*
> *Tan callando,*
> *cuán presto se va el placer,*
> *cómo después de acordado*
> *Da dolor,*
> *Cómo a nuestro parecer*
> *Cualquiera tiempo pasado*
> *Fue mejor.*
> *Nuestras vidas son los ríos*
> *Que van a dar a la mar*
> *Que es el morir, etc.*

Anyway, I won't bore you with further details of this humdrum moment in my life. My companion, Ingrid, was seduced by my writing and decided to have me dry out in the Eastern Pyrenees. That was the last time I ever saw Gouri, when I said goodbye to him on my doorstep, gifting him one of those Bibles people often steal from by-the-hour hotels. Now I'm married and the proud father of blonde triplets who look just like their mother. I've stopped drinking. I'll cede the floor to the rat again, underscoring once more that these letters were penned a year after the ones above. I will, quite presumptuously, name this part of the story "The New World."

Master, my silence must be worrying you. So many things have happened since that memorable night when the Rat Devil left us that I haven't found a single free moment to write them down for you. The next morning, we were awakened by the exceptionally excited albatross, who had smelled land during the night and flew away from the island, soaring high enough to make out, at dawn, a line encrusted in the horizon; it was an island much larger than our own, surely a continent, and we advanced toward it, driven forth by the wind. It was likely inhabited; in any case, we could see the green of nature's equatorial vegetation, or so the albatross thought, and trees require all sorts of creatures to survive in these regions. "It must be my emirate," the parrot claimed. The snake, having digested the iguana, and looking very much like him now, came to greet us with a somewhat forced smile and asked us what had happened in the meantime. No one took the time to tell him anything, each already busy with his own affairs. Rakä, noticing that the archbishop's compass had stopped turning, tried to find our location on a world map that had thankfully escaped the orgy of book burning. The Queen of Rats and her daughters, the princesses, were shaking out the archbishop's lavender sheets; the crumbs from Mimile's numerous sandwiches were keeping them awake. The Emir of Parrots decided to take his leave and go ashore on the wings of the albatross to survey the situation, he said, when in fact he simply wanted to leave as soon as possible because he had stolen the archbishop's amethyst cuff links, a crime the Queen accused him of; he calmly replied that the cuff links did not belong to us either, and that he had taken them not in order to sell but rather to wear himself; we weren't sure how to reply and we decided to make a gift of them. In the end, he decided to stay with us until we docked, too afraid to arrive in an unknown land without an escort. Rakä noticed that this continent did not appear on the maps, but perhaps the bishop's world map was ancient, predating the discovery of the Americas; perhaps we had found ourselves in a past or future time unrecorded by any human document (this was my secret desire). We couldn't distinguish the blue and green waters of the Pacific and Atlantic Oceans anymore, which had mixed together during the flood; the water shimmered in every shade from dark blue to gold, and the waves' crests were whitish-pink and orange; it was impossible to know where we were. Mimile, already drunk, celebrated the New World in his own special way: he dressed Vidvn up in the frocks of the Virgin from the altar of Notre-Dame, all dusty and surely infested with germs. Vidvn giggled in front of the archbishop's mirror, strutting her stuff. Rakä and I went down to the island to wake up the humans and rats and tell them the news. They all erupted with joy and we held a mass (Mimile and Vidvn officiated after one of my brief sermons) on the Parvis Notre-

Dame. The Queen had gotten all spruced up, sporting the human queen Marie Antoinette's blonde wig, which she had dug up from the archives of the Conciergerie. A few seals and sea lions came up onto the Parvis to join the mass, in which Mimile extolled the Rat Devil's benevolence and the New World's beauty. The baby seals and young rats played basketball with a makeshift ball, completely uninterested in the mass; the humans, lying in the sun, took their clothes off. Soon we could see land clearly. Standing before a spit of coral-yellow sand strewn with shells of golden brown sea snails stood a forest of trees of a size and kind we'd never encountered before, with trunks of every shade from sepia to red, the branches healthy and high, holding up fans of leaves as large as sails, and the fruit, ah, Master, the fruits that hung from those trees! I wouldn't trade a single one for all the Emir's jewels! They were of all shapes and colors and as luminous as if suns were stashed inside them instead of seeds and pits. The Île de la Cité, driven forth by a cool wind, slid gently onto the sands of the beach; we ran to lash the island's buildings to the mainland trees, the men pulling the ropes and the rats tying the knots. Some of us stayed aboard so we could cut them in case of attack, in order to protect the Court. The snake, displeased by our leadership during his downtime, joined forces with the parrot to protest our inefficiency. "If my escort were here, we'd have moored much more quickly," said the Emir, who received a good slap from Rakä, whereupon he angrily withdrew to consult with the snake in the Palais de Justice, where the albatross was standing guard at the door. This cracked up the men and rats, whose outspoken optimism, inspired perhaps only by exercise and the sea air, exceeded all bounds. A human, once condemned for having set fire to the forest of Fontainebleau, tried to set the forests of the New World ablaze, as well; I had to confiscate his matches and, thankfully, these humans knew nothing about rubbing stones together or using magnifying glasses to make fire; I was unable, however, to prevent them from chopping down a large tree, out of which they carved a pirogue to explore the shores of the continent which promised no shortage of abandoned cities to be plundered. Our rats, under the humans' influence, had become craven and power-hungry. Several expeditions were organized: the Emir of Parrots stood at the prow of the pirogue, the albatross at the stern, some twenty men, and two hundred rats to explore the southern part of the continent; the parrot had assured them that we were in the Caribbean and that he had all of Captain Drake's treasure maps, the snake led a line of men followed by a column of rats, who went into the forest with provisions and rifles on their heads in search of El Dorado. Very few of us stayed behind to build our City. Apart from a few madwomen from Sainte-Anne and a handful of Russian sailors, only two salt-and-pepper seals and three fairly old American drug offenders stayed behind with us. One of them was an engineer and advised us to move Notre-Dame onto the mainland, as its weight was causing the island to sink further and further, and the salt water was eroding its cement, which had already been battered by the violence of the waves, and almost ruined by human violence; we saw no point in it. "Our City," I replied, "will be built with our paws, our hearts, our tails, and our snouts," and a number of rats applauded me. Peter (for that was the engineer's name) shrugged his shoulders and lit a cigarette he'd rolled with the Indian hemp that grew freely among the tree roots, intermingled with mushrooms and parsley, before turning and walking quietly away along the beach until he had disappeared on the horizon. In a single day, an old Russian sailor dismantled an ancient house stone by stone behind the Cathedral and rebuilt it on a sand dune, and the other humans, following his example, did much the same, but crafted themselves more cramped and hurried dwellings, some just pits in the sand. We rats took possession of a tree beside which our old willow paled in comparison, its slimmest roots being thicker than the willow's entire trunk, on which we set up the ancient furniture from the archbishopric of Paris, the heaviest of which was the four-post bed with Vidvn and Mimile still asleep on it, likely dead drunk and impossible to remove. The next step was to make sure we had fresh water, which fortunately was just a stone's throw away, falling cool and clear in a pretty cascade over our new home's roots. We let our wives and their mother oversee the move into the new tree, and Rakä and I, after a brief discussion, set off in search of the stream's source; the silence of the virgin forest troubled us: no earthly creature made a sound. The roots of these trees were gigantic and exuded a sweet resin not dissimilar to honey, which we tasted and found exquisite. A mere hundred yards from our tree we found the source of our fresh water: it trickled out of a pyramid of round pebbles. "Not a soul in sight," said Rakä. I concurred: all the land mammals, apart from us, had perished in the disaster. The silence was troubling; we could hear the stream and the chilly wind, but nothing living. The volunteer rats who made up our escort joined us, bringing us a cup of linden tea on the Queen's behalf, reporting that they had ventured a little way up the coast and had found the same: not a soul in sight. We all sat down on a root and stared at each other, dumbstruck. The rats who had stayed behind with us introduced themselves by name: Jerry, Pöoul, and Domino. We weren't worried for our survival, far from it, given the abundance of edible vegetation, including the roots, which tasted like chocolate; and for the carnivores there were fish from the sea and trout from the stream. The Queen of Rats came to join us with a tray of medlars. She complained about her ever-intractable daughters and the two salt-and-pepper seals (apparently an old couple) who wouldn't stop playing ball with a melon in front of our tree, flinging sand in everyone's eyes. We returned to the beach to observe a squadron of silver dolphins, just off the coast; the humans were tossing bananas into their open mouths. When they saw us they stopped their game, as if guilty. Rakä stepped forward to welcome the dolphins and, being afraid of rats, they swam away in formation. The humans also returned to their homes and dens, leaving us alone on the beach. Alone again, us rats, as usual. We decided unanimously that this was not the place for us, grabbed some sweaters and matches, and headed off into the forest in search of a valley where we could build our City without them, bidding farewell to Vidvn and Mimile, who were weighing us down (and we them), wishing all the same to see them again someday, to learn of each other's lives, with tears in our eyes.

The Magic Mushrooms

WE WOVE THROUGH THE ROOTS OF THE TREES IN SINGLE file; Rakä led the way, using the scimitar the Emir of Parrots had forgotten on the sand as a machete to hack away the vines blocking our path. I followed him, holding up my wife, Carina, who complained of pain in her lower abdomen, crying miscarriage, her sister Iris let herself be carried on the soldier Jerry's back, Jerry's backpack having been passed on to Pöoul, Domino followed along, carrying on his back a Préfontaines bottle full of fresh water, a gift from Mimile, and the Queen gathered pine nuts in her skirt, offering them around as she belted out the Marseillaise. Her excessive activity and eccentric behavior led me to suspect that she had entered menopause. We made our way upstream; the water was underground by this point, but if we pressed our ears to the ground, we could hear its sound with increasing clarity, like a waterfall we could hear distinctly in the air. It was almost noon and Rakä suggested we stop for a quick snack. The army rabble (Jerry, Pöoul, and Domino) took the opportunity to express their demands: food would soon run out and our wives were too tired to continue the journey. They agreed to escort us to the falls in exchange for the diamond on the Queen's crown, which she had traded with the Emir of Parrots for Marie Antoinette's wig, an item that would help him keep warm in his pirogue. We reluctantly agreed, saying that once we reached the waterfall we would hunker down for a few days to prepare for Iris and Carina's coming labor, and we would take advantage of this pretext to discharge the soldiers, whom we were beginning to mistrust. The Queen burned a pine cone, wrapping it in a trout she had brought in her underpants, and we drank fresh water and ate a few almonds. We were eager to arrive at the falls, the immensity of which we could hear ever more clearly, but the forest was getting thicker and thicker and the sun's rays had trouble weaving all the way down to us. We resumed our walk and I assumed machete duty, which quickly left me breathless. The Queen had the idea to climb the branches and move forward by clinging to the lianas, an idea we found brilliant, although we regretted all the time we had wasted digging tunnels, a relic of our rodent fear. We climbed to the top of a tree with a trunk that was as hard as an oak and topped with bamboo canes that held up fan-shaped palm leaves quivering in the breeze, fully illuminated by the sun; cherries as big as watermelons hung from the end of the bamboo shoots entwined with beautiful lianas that swayed like living ropes and on which we swung most pleasurably. The waterfall was close by, whipping the water below like a head of hair, the way a gypsy woman shakes her crystal locks, as it came crashing down over two great, round boulders. Rakä and I moved ahead by jumping from branch to branch or clinging to the vines, and our wives Iris and Carina, being afraid of heights, rode on our backs. I cannot possibly describe the beauty of this waterfall to you, Master, only its dimensions: ten thousand human feet tall, with at least thirty stories of gigantic trees dipping their roots in the water, it fed a river so wide that it was difficult to see the opposite shore, and which reached the ocean, far behind us now, at the delta. We got fairly close, although we feared the clouds of mist rising up from the foot of the falls and the water's deafening noise. Evening was falling and we decided to settle down in a clearing inside a travel bag and all fell asleep after enjoying the sunset, eating some red mushrooms with white polka dots, which sprang up all around us, with a vinaigrette. Rakä woke me abruptly. Our soldiers had left us in the middle of the night, taking everything with them, not only our food but almost all our clothes, as well; the Queen snored naked in the moonlight and our two wives were curled up in a ball beside her. "Those filthy bastards!" I cried, and Rakä hushed me, placing his paw over my mouth. I focused my ears and thought I heard, behind the noise of the waterfall, a sort of animal moaning, although it was impossible to tell what was making it. We covered the Queen and our wives, who went on snoring, with a shirt Mimile had given us and tiptoed to the shore of the river fed by the falls. Except for the light of the moon shimmering on the water, the entire landscape was as still as ever; a light breeze rustled through the treetops and we could smell the distant sea. The moaning, if it wasn't a figment of our imagination, had stopped. "The silence is making us hear voices," said Rakä when we heard footsteps brushing against the vegetation around us, but we saw nothing; we huddled together, trembling in fear. The branch of a large tree snapped sharply and came crashing down beside us; the moaning resumed, as if on cue. We thought we saw a shiny object glisten on the river, and suddenly a great wind broke out, pushing the falls aside as easily as a lock of hair, and rain began pouring down; the downpour didn't even last a minute, but the rain had been so abundant that we found ourselves soaked and wading through mud. We felt the wing of an invisible bird brush against us and the clouds parted, unveiling the roundest and most luminous moon that had ever existed. We thought we saw a few forms taking shape in the air; they rustled like dead leaves as they brushed together. A murmur like a prayer soon arose from among them as they took on a more precise form, but as we focused our eyes and ears we realized that the apparitions and murmurs were coming in all different shapes and languages, a combination of all animal forms and their wailing and tongues, but the overall sound was like the waterfall's, only more plaintive. Soon they were grouping together on the surface of the river; hordes of them descended from the trees on both banks of the river and many more came soaring in, becoming ever more distinct, each more monstrous than the last. And so we saw, from our hiding place under a stone, as our hair bristled with terror upon our scalps, a pig-faced tuna with a mule's head, an elephant with a human head whose trunk ended in a giant fingernail, a turkey-headed toad with a peacock's tail, a griffin exactly as they're described, a woman with a kangaroo's head and tail carrying a large rooster-headed scorpion in her pouch, and among them the God of Man, but with a lizard's tail and two heads (a poodle's and a fox terrier's) in place of his own, and I could go on with even more uncanny examples, such as a sea turtle with a fish tail for a head. Their bodies and litanies became ever clearer; they covered the entire river (one wonders by what contrivance they stood level with its surface), all facing the falls. We thought they must have been asking the waterfall for something, each pronouncing a unique list, likely reciting a different dictionary. A light began to develop behind the waterfall: a cloud of a thousand and one colors from which the sun suddenly emerged like a ball hurled into the sky. The shades were literally frozen in midair by a sudden icy wind that blew in from the sea, and they fell, breaking away like great lumps of ice, into the river, the current of which carried them out to sea at the same time that the waterfall stopped flowing, as if someone had turned off a giant faucet. All was silent and still. As the river gently drained away, a city was revealed, most likely human, almost completely enclosed within the hollow of the falls, which we decided to explore later, once the water in the riverbed had receded enough to let us advance through the mud. When the moon's disc crossed the sun, passing in front of it to reach the horizon above the ex-waterfall, everything went black again for a moment; then as the sun reappeared we saw the Emir of Parrots flying in zigzags, crossing the river and shouting: "Wait for me! Wait for me!" We had no plans to run away. He landed, banging his head against a tree as usual, trembling with fear, and told us, "We're in Hell!" We calmed him down as best we could and returned with him to our camp to wake up our wives for a light morning snack. We told the Queen of Rats about our adventure, hiding it from our wives—who certainly would have been taken aback—but the Queen was not concerned at all: she had dreamed the very same thing without needing to travel to the river, she replied. We decided that these beings, even if they returned—and whatever they were—meant us no harm; in the end, we even found them comical, as we recalled their physical deformities and their voices.

The City of Rats

THE EMIR OF PARROTS KISSED THE QUEEN OF RATS familiarly on both sides of her whiskers before bursting into tears on her shoulder. "I've lost a leg," he wailed, and indeed he had, though he managed to hop around with ease on the remaining one by leaning on his wings. Rakä made him a prosthesis, carving a little branch we all agreed was quite becoming, which he adorned with a small emerald ring, the only precious stone he had managed to save from his misadventure by hiding it in his rectum. Our wives came back from the river complaining that it had run dry, we pointed out a small stream where they could wash up and they got angry, saying it wasn't as pretty. We were eagerly awaiting the birth of our children, not so much to see them but in the hope that maternity might sweeten their mothers' characters. The Queen prepared us a cup of rubber milk and honey, which the parrot sucked down almost single-handedly through a straw, before he began to speak. "As soon as we were at sea," he said, "we were boarded by an army of dolphins, and believe me when I tell you that these animals are diabolically cunning. At first they claimed that they would escort us to an abandoned Mayan city built entirely of gold, on the far side of the mouth of a delta; the men rowed like galley slaves and the rats ran all over the place, operating the archbishop's violet cassock as a makeshift sail. We started to worry when we saw the dolphins multiplying to both starboard and port; at one point a good thousand of them were leaping perilously over our pirogue, almost tipping it over, when we realized that they were leading us out into the open sea, where the strong wind tore off our sail. Several poor rats, clinging to it, were tossed into the air and soared a few dozen yards before sinking into the waves where the dolphins played with them like toys, throwing them back and forth, twirling them around by the tail. Laughter marked all of their faces as they flashed their little triangular teeth under their cretinous eyes." "We have to help them!" cried Rakä. "Too late," murmured the Emir. "They're all dead!" "The humans too?" "Not the humans," said the parrot. "We got lucky because a gang of sharks swooped in on the dolphins, who swam up the river delta (sharks need more depth to turn around), escaping but not without leaving a few corpses in their wake. We managed to make it back to shore, rowing against the current, exhausted, night already fallen; the madwoman from Sainte-Anne who had come along as our barracks bunny had died of fright in the meantime and we buried her before lying down in a hole in the sand. And that's when things really went downhill: The men, aroused by their day at sea, wanted sex; a group of them dug up the mental patient to desecrate her sand-strewn corpse; five others took hold of the albatross and shoved a beer bottle up his anus while choking him, then they took turns raping him while he thrashed his wings." "And you, Emir?" "I was weeping," he sobbed, "they had chained one of my legs to a tree. At night, once they had roasted the albatross and the mental patient over a huge bonfire on the beach and devoured them, I pecked off my own leg with my beak in order to escape, and left it hanging from the end of the chain." "Damn them to hell!" cried Rakä. The anguish I felt was comparable to the day when the God of Man told us about their stay in Eden. "So they haven't changed," I said to myself. "And what about the rats?" I exclaimed, shocked that, in my anxiety, I'd thought of them last of all. "The surviving rats scattered into the forest," replied the Emir, and as if in echo to his reply we heard rats squeaking: "Hee! Hee! Hee!" They rushed toward us from among the trees, shouting: "The humans are coming!" Our wives and the Emir panicked; we calmed them down with a few smacks. "Run for the city behind the waterfall!" ordered Rakä, and we bounded behind him on all fours, hastily grabbing some of our food and rags. The riverbed was almost dry now but still a bit muddy, and so rushed was our flight that we slipped right over it, crashing into each other; the Emir followed us, hopping on his one claw, his wooden leg lost, shouting "Wait for me!" The human City, as we approached, seemed less and less human to us; built into the dried-out river mud, it was composed of several levels, laid out in a spiral or near spiral, a straw roof, still damp as if it had been carelessly tossed on top, perhaps cast there by chance in the storm, and a ruined tower stood above it, one destroyed section of which revealed several habitations linked by staircases. I was astonished by the lower floors, which looked as if they had been constructed for dinosaurs, while the upper floors, successively more cramped, could scarcely accommodate a creature of our size. As we approached the city, we watched it rise higher and higher, its upper levels obscured by the clouds over the falls, and it was much further away than we'd thought. We arrived breathless at the foot of the City, carrying our fainting wives in our arms;

at its entrance, our friend the snake was impatiently eyeing a wristwatch tied to the end of his tail, which he had stolen, or so he claimed, from an Indian. He greeted us sternly: "Where have you been? I've been looking all over for you since this morning. See how I was first to find the City of Rats?" And above the main entrance we saw the letters RATS written in troglodyte characters. This wasn't exactly our idea of what the City would be like, but there was no time to lose. According to the snake, who was very sensitive to the vibrations of the earth, the humans were approaching the river's source in closely grouped ranks, having linked up with the ones who had left him for dead after choking him and tearing off his skin to make a whip out of it; fortunately, he had several layers, each more beautiful than the last. We followed him through the entrance, unnerved by the lack of a drawbridge. "Don't worry about that," he said, "the first few floors are made up of labyrinths, all of which lead to a cave under the City that's so deep it reaches the center of the earth; I've already explored the whole thing." And we rats immediately felt reassured, accustomed as we were to weaving through labyrinths (and this one was a model of its kind), combining every possible kind of corridor at various levels and of all dimensions; the Emir of Parrots got lost behind us in the meanders and the snake had to come to his rescue. Soon we were about fifty yards above the ground (to count in terms of stories is impossible, given the City's irregularity) and we came out onto a hexagonal plaza with a stream of water at its center that trickled down in silence, surrounded by several stone benches and geraniums, and we ran toward a balustrade with a view over the delta; the men advanced, swaying and disorganized, along the riverbed. The Queen passed me her binoculars; there were indeed two thousand or more humans, nearly all survivors from the old Île de la Cité; we, however, were a mere hundred rats, and even though the majority of us were exhausted and sick, we all swore to fight to the bitter end; every one of us wielded either a razor blade or glass shard. That's when I saw Mimile walking ahead of their crowd, with Vidvn in his arms, the others whipping him forth with the snake's skin. Our two wives Iris and Carina had taken ill and were suffering the first contractions; we laid them down beside the water fountain where the Emir of Parrots assured us that he would care for them, having overseen several births before. Our hundred rats raced down to the City gates and, as a precaution, erected a mountain of round stones to block the entrance. Meanwhile, the Queen inspected the upper floors and said she'd found some excellent frescoes in the style of the Cave of Altamira depicting long-haired rats, most likely our ancestors who, according to our legends, hailed from Atlantis. The humans were soon at the gate, kicking Mimile down to his knees with their boots while he shielded Vidvn with his arms and head. One of them shouted: "Rat bastards! You had the map of the City and you let us drown in the swamps and kill each other, open the door or I'll blow Mimile's head off!" I gulped. And I uttered these atrocious words: "The door is always open to you." Here, the snake passed me a shot of alcohol for courage, and I went on: "This City does not belong to us. But the door is blocked by stones and a labyrinth lies within." They violently shoved Mimile out of the way, and he stumbled off to take refuge with Vidvn under a tower, and here is the shortsighted action that led to their ruin, which my experience had taught me to foresee. They rushed (as, perhaps, they always do) to remove the pebbles from the entrance and threw themselves into the labyrinth. "Well," said the snake, consulting his wristwatch, "we won't be seeing them any time soon!" In no time at all we heard them running through the dark corridors, crashing into each other and screaming in lamentation all through the night. We invited Mimile to climb up a rope ladder; he cried back to us through his swollen mouth, spitting out the last of his teeth: "Thank you, rats!" and Vidvn waved goodbye (I thought she looked a bit melancholic) before they walked away along the riverbed, fading into the sunset over the delta. In the meantime, our wives had given birth; the parrot, in his nervousness, had placed our respective litters into the same hat; we never did know which child was whose, but what does it matter. In the night, a human managed to conquer the labyrinth's geometry and reach our terrace; we chased him off with stones and he fled screaming back into the cellars. The moon rises and we're safe. The Queen gave our princesses dandelion water lavages, excellent, she said, for putting them to sleep. The parrot could not stop admiring the beauty and intelligence of our offspring, which clung indifferently to their two mothers' teats. The snake curled up to sleep on a City column topped with a statue so eroded by nature and the elements that we couldn't tell what it represented. The Queen of Rats, who had taken a fancy to the Emir of Parrots, was reciting Milton's *Paradise Lost* to him and fanning herself with a large geranium leaf, seated by the fountain. Rakä and I worked up a great red wine and lentil stew for us and our hundred rat soldiers. They swore that they would guard the

Court of Rats against any unlikely human attack while Rakä and I, making use of the moon already high in the sky, ventured up to the highest floors of the City, intrigued by its cool, silent, silvery gloom.

The Return to Land

HAVING LEFT OUR COMPANIONS DOZING IN PEACE, RAKÄ and I struggled our way out onto the dimly moonlit cobblestones of a street that led to another, and another, and so it went, on and on; the streets ran into each other diagonally and tended, per Rakä's estimation, toward a common destination; we tried to avoid the cross streets, which ran in parallel circles or spirals. "We've been climbing for hours," Rakä said, "and haven't found a thing." At one street corner, however, we heard a disconcerting noise and hid in a stone recess. It was just an empty, harmless tin of tomato sauce rolling over the cobblestone; we held our breath and let it roll past. "The City seems deserted," Rakä whispered to me, "there's nothing for us here, Gouri; let's go back!" I realized that he was afraid to climb any higher and told him that I'd go on alone if I had to. "Gouri," Rakä said, clutching my hands, "we're alive and safe for now, let's just go back—please! We have wives now, they just gave birth to healthy little rats tonight, I'm begging you, Gouri!" And as I turned around to look him in the eye, he lowered his eyelashes and dashed off down the stairs. But he came running back at full speed and said: "Till death do us part, brother!" and we each kissed the other's ears. We kept on climbing and came to an octagonal plaza, a sort of cloister; at the center of each wall was an opening that may or may not have, in some remote time, concealed a door: irregular ovals two feet off the ground, leading to vaulted grottoes whose walls were covered in a thousand layers of paintings and inscriptions, discernible only by the moonlight streaming in through gaps in the sections of stone that had crumbled over time; it was then that we understood that this city had been inhabited by rats for millions of years. On the wall of the first cave we visited was a drawing, practically intact, of the profile of the very first rat, who had only three whiskers and was otherwise bald. His tail ended in a snake's head. And these words had been carved into the stone, over the image: "'We paide a greate price when we gave up our Freedom,' said the Storke, 'thus were we forced to sacrifyce our Equalitie.' And she looked as if lost in a Dreame. The Frogge shook her Legge, that she myghte continue her Speeche, but she sayde Naught. The Frogge understoode that the Storke was pondering Inceste then was swallowed whole." We passed through a tunnel into the next cell, its vault so low that its ceiling brushed our ears; the hole that led out to the open air was covered with a grill, but the bars, twisted and polished, suggested that it had been inhabited recently. In a corner, we found an old bear paw, hollowed out and molded into the shape of a human foot, and a man's headdress fashioned out of an alligator's head on which someone had affixed buffalo horns. And everything was stained with animal excrement of every sort, although it was so old that it no longer smelled, blending in perfectly with the other objects, paintings, and inscriptions. We didn't enter the other cells; they were too dark. At the center of this cloister was a well, which would have been quite easy to fall into by accident; we leaned over it carefully. Far below us, we saw our two wives and twenty children sleeping in a ball on Mimile's old shirt; the Queen of Rats, nestled in the Emir of Parrots' wings, was snoring beside them, and we listened to the echoes of their entwined snores bouncing off the rocks. All around them, on the red and white checkered floor, our hundred soldier rats slept in disarray; the snake, possibly suffering from insomnia, whistled as he slithered in quick circles around the lip of the Andalusian fountain at the patio's center, where, leaning over again, we managed to glimpse a much deeper section of the labyrinth lit by moonlight where a few men were crawling around, feeling blindly at the walls or climbing up with great effort, only to fall back down into the neighboring corridor which led inexorably back to the same place. I shuddered and clutched Rakä's paw. "What have we done?" I whispered. He wrapped his tail around my shoulders and said: "Nothing, Gouri, everything's happening of its own accord.* Let's go back down, I don't like these upper floors in the dark; let's wait until sunrise; tomorrow we'll go up higher." But the moon was almost at its peak and we had nothing to fear from a vacant city. He answered: "Till death do us part, brother," and followed me into a narrow, never-ending spiral staircase; through the holes in the walls, every two or three stories, we could see the horizon line over the falls, behind an immense desert of sand. The higher we climbed, the vaster the continent appeared. The great desert that dominated it was speckled with forests, woods, lakes, seas, mountains and cordilleras; we were certain that it was completely uninhabited: nothing moved. We came to a narrow, golden door encrusted with shimmering stones of every color; it was locked, just barely

---

* I repeat to the reader that I am translating without adaptation. —Tr.

big enough for us to fit through, and redolent of musk. The key lay on the ground beside it. "Don't open it, Gouri," Rakä cried. Exasperated, I called him a coward and opened the door. We emerged into a long, narrow chamber divided by a small subterranean river where a few chicken feathers and the viscera of a fish drifted by; above the river, water trickled out of a rectangular metal grate, through which we were able to pull ourselves up, with me climbing onto Rakä's shoulders, then lifting him up by the tail. We found ourselves in a place that seemed familiar, although we were unable to say why; it looked like our sewer on Carrefour de Buci, though it was longer according to Rakä, and shorter in my opinion. There was a large opening that led out to a noisy area that was unquestionably inhabited, we ran straight toward it. We saw a rubber-soled basketball shoe stamping out a cigarette and a grayish pigeon hopping toward us. "Been a while since you opened your shop," he said, shaking his head, "watch out or you'll lose all your customers; a couple of yellow Hare Krishna rats opened a stand just like yours on the corner of Rue Mazet." And we heard the Rat Devil's enormous laugh ring out like a jackhammer. We rushed, frightened, back into the sewer in search of the City gate; in its place we found a very young rat with red eyes shivering in the cold, who stammered: "The gate is closed!" We understood that it was one of our sons who had slipped away from his mothers' watchful gaze and followed us on our exploration of the City. The little rat leapt to my neck, crying with fright. We had a hard time comforting him, as we weren't used to babies; after lengthy cuddling, he fell asleep, suckling Rakä's whiskers. We told each other that perhaps, since he had come into the world during our adventure, he wouldn't make the same mistake as we had in adventuring into the world, although, even as we racked our brains, we couldn't figure out what mistake we had actually made. Unsure whether he was Rakä's son or mine, and seeing that he bore a striking resemblance to his grandmother, the Queen of Rats, we decided to name him Gourakäqueen, an amalgam of our three names, omitting his two harpy mothers, who, we thought, Gourakäqueen and we would be better off without, a fact that helped us miss the New World a bit less. "He'll be an adventurous lad," said Rakä; "As soon as he was born, he followed us all those miles up the steep slope out of pure curiosity. So," he concluded, "this week-long interlude in our lives will have been good for something, after all: we share a son who resembles us in spirit." I thought that this might not be the ideal education for a young rat, but I kept this to myself. "Let's trust in his wits," said Rakä, as if he'd read my mind.

Au revoir, Master. Until the next letter. Your Gouri.

Translator's afterword

AND THAT WAS THE LAST LETTER I RECEIVED FROM OUR friend Gouri. I was a little surprised by the abrupt ending, but perhaps it was inevitable, given how hard the author had tried to remain faithful to the description of a reality that sometimes works against him. Surely, I could have reworked this last letter to leave Gouri off in a better position (as emperor of the New World, for example), but I opted to publish them exactly as I received them, leaving it to the reader's discretion whether to draw any moral or conclusion from them.

The poem cited on page 89 belongs to the Castilian soldier Jorge Manrique (1440–1479), the first stanza and the beginning of the second of "Coplas a la muerte de mi padre," which I consider impossible to translate into French (or into modern Spanish, a language I also know) because its rhymes so nearly approach perfection. It recounts the last moments of the soldier's father; the poet uses this event as an example to lead the reader to reflect on the fleeting nature of our lives, comparing them to rivers that "flow to the sea"—a stand-in for "dying."

As for the madwomen of Sainte-Anne's mental asylum, I don't know what misunderstanding led Gouri to place that institution within the geography of the Île de la Cité, he may have confused it with the Cité metro station (about which, on the other hand, he hardly says a word). I thought it would be useful to cut some of my notes, the erudition of which surpasses and cancels out the imagination, out of respect for the author's style, which I wanted to keep fluid and fresh. Even so, I would like to make one final comment that my role as human translator permits me (in this particular case and seeing as it concerns a rodent author): I personally don't believe this story is true, especially when I compare it to many imaginative works from my children' s library. Our blonde triplets (Sylvie, Rebecca, and Djémilla) simply adore the passage about the fox terrier in his waxed tartan raincoat and the one about the Queen of Rats belting out the Marseillaise, which motivated me to keep them here, thinking that perhaps, in time, this tale would become a children's book; I've asked one of my wife Ingrid's friends to illustrate it to that effect. Another touch of personal history that, as an honest man of letters, I cannot suppress: As soon as I had finished this translation—which, believe me, required a great deal of concentration, since Gouri's handwriting is so bad, not to mention his syntax, spelling, and other such details—I fell fast asleep on my manuscript. My wife Ingrid came to wake me up on tiptoes so I could go sleep in my own bed (we live in a cute little pavilion in Sète), I woke up and thought I saw the Rat Devil's head on my wife Ingrid's shoulders. Our triplets, awakened by my screams, ran into the library; on my daughter Rebecca, I saw the head I had always imagined for Rakä: with a protruding muzzle and enormous ears sticking out of her skull, on her sister Sylvie a snake's head and a long forked tongue, and on Djémilla the head of the Emir of Parrots— even her voice was the same. Understanding that I was going through a fit of delirium due to nervous exhaustion, I closed my eyes and hid under my desk, asking loudly for them to leave me alone in the library with a blanket and my wife's pill bottle of Valium; once I'd slept a few hours, my vision was sure to return to normal. (I'd had similar, albeit less serious, accidents in my alcoholic past.) But by the next morning my condition had worsened: I thought I was at the center of a labyrinth that was my own home, in the hallways of which I struck my very own triplets with a broomstick while they played hopscotch; I wounded Rebecca (my favorite) in the head, in my delirium I saw her as a giant rat that was trying to attack me. My wife Ingrid had the presence of mind to call an ambulance and lock me away in the library. The nurses arrived in time to slap a straitjacket on me before I was able to destroy the books and shelves, which I was preparing to set on fire. They had me sleep for a week in the clinic, then I came home completely depressed, my head full of confused ideas. With this afterword, I would like to offer my sincerest gratitude to my wife Ingrid and my three daughters who were good enough never to mention these incidents again, even when I myself have brought them up in an attempt to apologize. My wife Ingrid and I decided to spend the Easter holidays in Paris. I took the opportunity to rest my jangled nerves and deliver this manuscript to my editor. We left the triplets with their grandmother in Sète. Walking out of my editor's office with check in pocket, I wrapped my arm around Ingrid's shoulder; we were happy as one is in Paris when springtime comes and two makes one; we walked to the Carrefour de Buci and went for a martini at Le Dauphin before grabbing lunch at Le Muniche, once the site of our first pledges of love. Gazing into her blue eyes, leaning on the counter and holding my jacket jauntily over my shoulder, I said to my wife: "This book feels good and done, darling," and breathed a sigh of relief. We burst out laughing. And with her inimitable pretty blonde pout, Ingrid brought her lips near mine as she plucked my publisher's check from my pocket, saying: "For my mink, darling," as I watched it disappear into her crocodile-skin handbag, which clicked shut. "So," I said to myself, "I've finally come back down to earth."

And with that: au revoir, as our dear rat once said. Your Copi.

VINTAGE CLASSICS

Vintage Classics is home to some of the greatest writers and thinkers from around the world and across the ages. Bringing you not just the books you already know and love, but new additions to your library, these are works to capture imaginations, inspire new perspectives and excite curiosity.

Renowned for our iconic red spines and bold, collectable design, Vintage Classics is an adventurous, ever-evolving list. We breathe new life into classic books for modern readers, publishing to reflect the world today, because we believe that our times can best be understood in conversation with the past.